THEIR CAPTIVATED BRIDE

BRIDGEWATER MÉNAGE SERIES - BOOK 3

VANESSA VALE

Cover design: Bridger Media

Cover photos: Period Images

GET A FREE BOOK!

1

CROSS

The first time I saw her I thought her a vision. In the lantern light of the hall, her hair was as black as pitch, artfully pulled back into a bun at her nape, but with loose, soft curls that made my eyes follow the graceful curve of her neck. Her skin had a golden glow to it, as if lit from within. Her pale blue dress was modest, yet hinted at every one of her curves, and those curves were quite appealing. I was not the only one who noticed them, for men's eyes turned her way as she danced, walked past or even smiled in their direction. It was her eyes though, that drew me in completely, for when she turned those pale blue eyes my way, I was lost.

She had the look that Rhys or Simon would call Black Irish: black hair and light blue eyes. I'd never met someone with the combination before and it was striking. In fact, I couldn't look away. The public dance in celebration of the country's independence was a well-attended affair, especially in a town the size of Helena. It wasn't often any of us from Bridgewater made it to this town; only ranch business brought us this far afield. Our ranch kept us well occupied and fairly self-sufficient. While Ian and Kane had made the last cattle contracts, it was our job— Simon, Rhys and I—to purchase a stud horse needed to improve already superior bloodline of Bridgewater's horses. It was one of our goals to make the sturdiest, fastest and best horses in the Montana Territory.

To hell with the horses. I wanted—no, needed—to know who this woman was. I couldn't leave the dance without hearing her voice or feeling her waist beneath my hand as we danced. I wanted to know her scent.

"Ask her to dance," Rhys said, coming up beside me. We didn't look at each other, but at the lovely woman who was right now sipping lemonade and speaking with two other women. The others were of similar age, perhaps early twenties, but neither even sparked my interest. Had I turned around and been quizzed as to their appearances, I doubt I could have warranted a fair guess. It was *she* who held my regard.

We stood on the outer fringes of the dance floor, the music— two violins, an accordion and a piano—not so loud here as to make speaking with others difficult. Several sets of doors were open to the cooler evening air and I saw one of *her* wayward curls shift in the breeze. I spared a glance at Rhys. He was taller than I by an inch or two, but trimmer of build. His hair was as dark as the mysterious woman's, yet his skin was much darker from time spent outdoors and natural inclination. He might look the part of a Montana man, but he was not born, nor bred, in the Territory, nor even the United States. He, as well as our other friend Simon, were both from the United Kingdom - Simon from Scotland and Rhys from England. In fact, the Englishman's name with the strange spelling had a simple pronunciation of Reese. Why it wasn't written as such was just another British anomaly I could never comprehend. One only had to hear the duo speak to know they were foreigners.

The woman smiled.

"You do not find her...."

I couldn't think of the right word.

"Unique?" Rhys asked. "I find her unique." That was true. She was unique that she had captured my attention, and it seemed his as well.

"Simon would think so as well if he were here instead of at his meeting," I considered. We were in Helena for the horse purchase, not a dance, but as it was decided that Rhys and I remain separate from the arrangement, we'd chosen to spend our idle evening at the town function.

"Meeting? It's a bloody game of Poker."

"Business arrangements are forged over liquor, women and cards."

"He may have the liquor and cards, but we have the woman," Rhys stated.

He was the quiet one of the three of us, a man of few words, but when he spoke those words were well chosen, and his statement was correct. Just looking upon this dark-haired beauty had me readily agreeing.

Simon, the Scot, was more brute strength than emotion and handled brash deals with ease. It was a good thing he was not here, for he would have knocked down everyone in his path to get to *her*, regardless of her married state or inclination towards foreign men. This method would have worked had we not been at a town dance; this environment took finesse and he was not known for that.

"She has not been with a specific man most of the evening, so I do not believe her to be claimed," I commented, placing my hands in the pockets of my pants. No man held her attention for long. Her smile, which was now given freely to the women she was with, was offered sparingly to men, and then only in a polite fashion. While I wouldn't pick up a woman and toss her over my shoulder like a caveman claiming his woman, I had no intention of idly standing by and watching the one I wanted slip through my fingers like sand. The band ended a song to scattered applause and I took the opportunity that presented itself. I approached her with my gaze fixed and when she saw me coming, it was as if she were trapped in a spider's web, unable to look away or move. The ladies at either side of her were still talking, however, she'd lost their attention in exchange for mine.

When I stopped beside her, the other ladies ceased their chattering and all three tilted their heads back to look up at me, for I was almost a head taller than all of them. I nodded at them in greeting, but kept my gaze fixed upon *her*. "May I have this dance?"

The band began to play a new tune and couples moved out onto the floor. Not wanting to give her an opportunity to say no, I took her hand in mine and led her out to an open spot. Perhaps I was part caveman after all. Her skin was warm, her fingers gripping mine. Turning to face her, I stepped in and placed my free hand on her waist to begin our dance. It fit in the delicate curve there, my little finger wedged against the flared bone of her hip, my large fingers almost touching the bumps of her spine. I could feel the stiff stays of her corset and wished I could instead learn the feel of her soft flesh. "My name is Cross," I said as I began to lead her around the dance floor. The steps were not complex and needed little to no thought as to the movement, which was well and fine, for my attention was focused squarely on her.

Her eyes had been on her hand at my shoulder, but she flicked a glance up at me. "I am Olivia. Olivia Weston."

I offered her a smile and her eyes widened in surprise. Was I that forbidding?

"Are you from Helena, Olivia?" I asked, hoping to make general conversation and set her at ease. I cut a formidable figure; I was taller than most and had thirty pounds on many a man. Women certainly looked at me twice, but often not because they were smitten, but fearful. The tight grip of her hand was the only indication as to any type of concern coming from Olivia, which was good, as I did not wish her to fear me. In fact, I wished her to find our dance quite pleasing, for I was enjoying holding her petite frame as I let her sweet scent entice me.

She gave a short nod, a curl bouncing as she did so. "Yes, and I assume you are not, for I believe I would have remembered you."

Her voice was soft, yet had almost a husky quality to it that had my blood stirring.

"I am that memorable then? That is good to know and quite a compliment," I replied.

"No, I mean...it's just--" she stuttered, then seeing the teasing gleam in my eye, pursed her mouth closed, although a corner tugged up and I knew no harm was done.

"I definitely would have remembered you, Olivia, if I had seen you before. In fact, I would have been quite attentive and you would not have forgotten me."

Her cheeks turned a pretty shade of pink and she gazed upon the buttons of my shirt.

"To answer your question, no. I hail from my ranch, Bridgewater, which is to the east of here."

She stiffened in my arms and at first, I thought it was the mention of Bridgewater, but then I took in that she was staring fixedly just beyond my left arm. She stepped in a touch closer and turned her forehead in toward my upper arm, as if using my body as some form of a shield.

"Something troubling you?" I asked, not looking in the direction that held her concern. While I maintained a calm demeanor and kept dancing, I was vigilant to any kind of bother or danger to Olivia.

She relaxed, forced a smile upon her face and replied, "No, everything is quite fine."

Something, no, probably someone, had bothered her, but she had no interest in sharing with me.

"We may have just met, but please consider me a protector, Olivia. I wish you no harm and I will see none come to you."

Surprise widened her pale eyes. "You say that as if you believe it."

"You don't think I can protect you?" Her words surprised *me*.

"Look at you." She indicated with a tilt of her chin. "You are...very large and could be quite an adversary."

I grinned again. "Yes, I am very large, and can put the size to good use." I doubted she understood my secondary meaning. "You have no male protector?"

"I live with my uncle, who is a dragon and protects me fiercely. I also do not lead an extravagant life and am in no need of much of a defender."

"Oh?" I replied neutrally.

"My uncle raised me and I have taken on his tendencies of educational pursuits, reading and remaining at home. I am fairly sheltered and not one for parties."

"You seem quite settled at this event," I countered.

She frowned briefly. "It is a holiday and besides, my uncle insisted."

"Then I will have to offer him my thanks."

"Why?" she asked, tilting her head slightly.

"I never would have met you otherwise and I am quite

pleased." Again, her cheeks flushed prettily. "But you never answered my question regarding a male protector."

"As I said, my uncle is quite enough. I am not in need of additional protection.'

From the way the men at the dance were watching her, I disagreed, but was not going to waste the dance arguing with her. I gave her hand a light squeeze so she looked to me. "Very well, but I am Cross from Bridgewater Ranch if you ever have need."

The song came to an end and while we stopped moving, I did not release her. "Promise me, Olivia."

People milled around us, chatting amiably while we stood still and I pinned her in place with my words.

"You are not in Helena and cannot offer any kind of shelter, regardless of the storm, however from the serious look upon your face, you will not release my hand until I agree."

I grinned at her savviness.

"Very well, I agree. I will call upon you if ever I have a time of need."

The definition of the word 'need' offered more than one connotation. While I would protect her from any type of harm, I also would gladly fill the role of any other kinds of needs she might have. From the look of her, from the type of rearing she had, she led a sheltered life and did not know of a woman's needs. The idea of any other man teaching them to her was off-putting at best.

Unfortunately, I had no choice but to release her. I was averse to do so for she felt..right in my arms.

2

OLIVIA

I had enough male interest to keep me dancing for most of the evening, which was quite surprising. From his place in the corner chatting with his friends, Uncle Allen watched with a broad smile. We'd wagered the last slice of cake that I would not be a wallflower at the event. Unfortunately for me, I was the loser and would not enjoy the dessert.

The attention was surprising, for my day-to-day life was quite tame. I had male callers, but none were of interest to me. Some were handsome even, but they spoke of insipid things as if I had an empty head. I did enjoy a discussion about ribbons and the latest dress patterns, but I also liked to engage in debates over statehood and other civic concerns. However, when I broached such a conversation, I was either rebuffed for not knowing my own head or scorned for sharing it.

It was Clayton Peters who had been subtle in his attentions but warranted the most concern. He was appealing to the eye, but his character set me on edge and made me feel quite uncomfortable. Each time I saw him, his attentions became more aggressive. He'd not physically touched me more than a shake of the hand; the aggression was verbal, proprietary. *When you are mine.... It is only a matter of time before you relent to my expectations.... My plans include you....*

He made my spine tingle and not in an appealing way. Although I rebuffed all of his attentions, he did not seem to recognize my disinterest or he did not care about it and continued to seek me out. Just a day earlier when we'd sat in my parlor and I'd told him I no longer wished to see him that he changed before my eyes. The attentive suitor was replaced by a man scorned - a sinister man who refused to take no for an answer. He was angry, his skin flushed and mottled, and he'd grabbed my wrist quite painfully until Uncle Allen hastily entered the room at the sound of our raised voices. He'd been stunned and angered by the other man's altered demeanor and had bodily removed him from the house.

After we'd calmed down—Uncle Allen vowing to 'kill the bastard' if Mr. Peters got anywhere near me again—he reminded me, "You will feel as if you were struck by lightning when you find the right man." That had never happened in my twenty-three years, especially not with Mr. Peters, and I started to feel concern that it never would. My uncle, while only in his early fifties, was a confirmed bachelor and clearly had not had such an occurrence, so I couldn't guarantee the veracity of his words. But at the dance it happened not once, but twice. Surely Uncle Allen was in error if I felt lightning two times within a short time span.

The first had been with the man named Cross. I wasn't sure if that was his given name or surname. He hadn't said, and my mind had not been clear enough to ask. To say the man befuddled me was an understatement. When I'd first seen him from across the room, I thought my heart had stopped for a moment, for it lurched, and then leapt against my breast and I felt hot all over. One time I'd fallen through a rotten board on the porch and I felt flustered and surprised and overheated and fearful and my heart had beat frantically at the jolt of it. Just looking into Cross's green eyes—for they most certainly were a very appealing grass green—had me feeling as if I'd fallen through the porch floor all over again. There had most definitely been a jolt.

He was tall enough where I only came to his chin. When I'd been in his arms for the dance I'd felt so small, his wide shoulders, solid torso and long legs had me ogling and from the closeness, it had been easy to do. His hand had dwarfed mine, all but swallowing it in his gentle grip. I'd expected him to be brash and rough, but he'd been just the opposite. I'd felt almost incorporated into his person, as if the rest of the dancers had disappeared and only a tall, fair-haired man existed. I could barely look past his shoulders. Instead, I had been content to get lost in his words, his deep voice, in his gaze. As he looked at me, I'd felt as if I had all of his attention, and perhaps I had. His jaw was square and his mouth wide beneath a long nose, yet it fit his face. His jaw was clean-shaven and his hair, while reasonably long, was neat and groomed.

When I'd glimpsed Mr. Peters in my periphery I had not wanted the dance to end. I'd felt safe and sheltered in Mr. Cross' hold, clearly protected from Mr. Peters' ire. Heat radiated from Cross' body, the clean, male scent of him enticing me to put my head upon his chest and close my eyes. Somehow, he'd noticed my fear over seeing the other man and offered his concern, even his protection. It had been...kind and I had wanted to revel in it, but the dance drew to an end, for then I worried if Mr. Peters would make a scene and I would have to deal with him once again, this time more publicly.

When Mr. Cross escorted me back to my friends, there was nothing more I could do than to thank him for the dance. Throwing myself at him or calling to him from across the room were things I could not do, regardless of the strength of my desire to do so. The lightning had struck and yet the man departed, and so did my eagerness to dance with others. Fortunately, I saw nothing more of Mr. Peters.

To my surprise, it was an hour later when the last dance was called, that lightning struck again. I was telling Uncle Allen that we could leave early, for nothing could compare to dancing with Mr. Cross, but a different man cleared his throat behind me. Uncle Allen saw him first and his eyes widened and a soft smile formed on his lips. I spun on my heel thinking it was Cross. Instead, it was the antithesis of him, but equally heart stopping. The newcomer had dark hair, perhaps as dark as mine, and tanned skin that only amplified the brightness of his smile. Dark eyes pinned me in place. Oh....

"Miss Weston, may I have this dance?" His voice was clipped, the words spoken with a strange accent.

Realizing my mouth was open, I snapped it shut. I glanced briefly at Uncle Allen, not wanting to put him out, yet at the same time didn't want him to see any hint of the jolt I felt at just the stranger's simple question, but he nodded readily.

"Yes, thank you," I replied.

He held out his elbow and I wrapped my hand around his biceps. His very thick, hard and well muscled biceps. The cut of his jacket did nothing to diminish it. As he led me out onto the floor, he leaned down closer so he could speak solely to me. "I am Rhys, a friend of a man you danced with earlier. Cross? Do you remember him?"

Remember? How could I have forgotten? But this man, he was so completely different than Mr. Cross. He was just as tall, but leaner. Darker, yet more intense. While Cross had been calm and offered his protection somewhat like a heavy winter blanket, Mr. Rhys was bright assurance and confidence. People parted for us; the man had a way about him that called for deference. When he took my hand in his he was just as gentle as Mr. Cross, but he had much more intent, placing my hand about his waist and the other upon my shoulder just as he wanted. When the music began and we started to move, I felt as if I was being taken for a dance rather than led.

As I glimpsed up at him through my lashes, I realized I'd been comparing instead of considering them separately. It wasn't as if I'd see Mr. Cross again, and there was certainly no reason for comparison. The men were different and just like Mr. Cross, when this dance ended I would not see Mr. Rhys again either. And so I stilled my thoughts and just enjoyed being held in the circle of his arms, knowing that he sought out the dance and had been interested specifically in my attentions.

"Miss Weston, it is rare to see a Black Irish such as yourself, and a quite lovely one at that," he commented. I'd heard the reference to my hair and eye color before, but that was not what made me misstep. A firm hand on my hip held me securely without a chance to fumble.

"How do you know my name?" I asked, cocking my head slightly.

The corner of his mouth tipped up. "As I said, Cross is my friend and he thought I might enjoy meeting you."

How strange. "Why?"

He frowned slightly and a small line formed at his brow. "Why?" he repeated. "It isn't often that either of us see such a beautiful woman, a woman who catches both of our eyes."

I couldn't help but flush at the compliment, but at the same time felt it odd. "You share dance partners?"

He took a moment before answering. "We share many things, Miss Weston."

Another odd answer, but I was intrigued. "Your friend, Mr. Cross, said that he was from a ranch east of here. Do you fare from that direction as well, for your accent is quite unique?" Surely it was idle chit-chat, but I didn't know what else to ask. He had me off kilter and the dance would end soon enough and that meant he would leave me just like his friend. It *was* just a dance. Nothing more.

"I am British, but I have not been there in some time. My home is Bridgewater, as is Cross'."

"Is it quite large?"

He arched a dark brow at my question, but responded easily enough. "I believe it to be one of the largest in the area, but we are a ranch of many."

"You are here in Helena on business or pleasure?"

"This dance and your company, Miss Weston, are all pleasure." The compliment heated my cheeks and I did not know how to respond, nor could I continue to look at him, so I studied the buttons on his dark jacket, just as I had with his friend. He was as neat as his friend. "We are in Helena to purchase a horse."

"You and Mr. Cross?"

The music played and the people danced around us but I, like before, ignored it all.

"Cross and I, as well as a good friend of ours, Simon."

"You have many friends," I added. I had many acquaintances, but no close, bosom friends.

"Not many, but the ones I do have I hold in the highest of esteem. And you? Your chaperone, Cross said he was your uncle?"

"Yes. My parents died when I was small and he raised me."

His hand tightened about my waist briefly. "I am sorry to hear about your parents."

A flicker of sadness appeared in his eyes was quickly hidden.

"You have lost family as well?" I ventured.

He gave a single nod. "I, unlike you, did not have an uncle to take me in and orphans are not held in the highest regard where I come from. Over time, I have learned that a family is one you make, so I have been lucky."

I faltered. "You are wed then?" I glanced around as if I could find a woman on the fringes of the dance that could be his wife. It was a silly act, but kept me from seeing the truth on his face.

"Of course not. I would not dance with another if I were married."

The dance drew to a close and Mr. Rhys led me back to my uncle, his hand upon the small of my waist. The feel of it sent tingles down my spine. Had I insulted him? A crushing feeling invaded my chest at the realization that I'd insulted his honor, for an honorable man would not seek out another woman for a dance or any other type of amusement.

"Sir." Mr. Rhys held out his hand to my uncle and introduced himself. "Thank you for the opportunity to dance with your niece."

"Anytime, young man," he replied. He seemed impressed by Mr. Rhys and was not aware of the gaffe I had made. "You are not from around here."

He shook his head. "No, sir. I am from Bridgewater."

Uncle Allen's face changed then, in some slight way I couldn't identify, but it wasn't disdain. He was...pleased somehow. Impressed, too. "I am familiar with another gentleman from the ranch, a Mr. Kane, I believe."

The dark slash of Mr. Rhys' brows rose in surprise. "Yes, Kane is part of Bridgewater as well."

"He purchased cattle last year from a man in Simms, I believe," Uncle Allen added.

"He did." He paused, then grinned. "Weston, yes. Now I have the connection. They were your cattle then."

Uncle Allen nodded.

"We are in town to purchase a stud horse, however the arrangement has not been as smooth as Kane's dealings with your man last year."

"Oh? Who is your connection here in Helena?"

"Clayton Peters. While he has been somewhat difficult to work with, his horse flesh is quite impressive."

I stiffened at the mention of his name.

"We are quite familiar with Mr. Peters," Uncle Allen said darkly. The curt tone and stiffness in his shoulders were not missed by Mr. Rhys.

"Is there something we should know about the man as part of our dealings? Has he treated you wrongly?"

To my surprise, Uncle Allen took my hand in his. "I have much respect for the men of Bridgewater, and of your ways, so I will share something with you." He lifted my hand and tugged the lace cuff of my dress back to show the bruises Mr. Peters had inflicted.

Mr. Rhys' eyes narrowed and his jaw clenched as he looked at the dark marks about my wrist. "Peters?" When I didn't answer, he looked to my uncle, who nodded. "Did he hurt you in any other way?" he asked me.

The vehemence and anger in his gaze had me stepping back, but I could not move from my uncle's gentle hold. I was embarrassed at my weakness being shared with a stranger and I covered my wrist with my other hand. "No, just wounded my pride," I replied.

"I am in town with Cross, whom you met, Miss Weston, as well as Simon McPherson. If there is anything you need, please do not hesitate to contact any one of us, now or at Bridgewater."

"Thank you," Uncle Allen replied. "These two men, they are of like minds as you?"

A look passed between the men but I did not know what it was. Mr. Rhys nodded and replied, "Indeed." The man turned to me and offered slight bow. "Miss Weston, the pleasure was mine. I hope to make your acquaintance again soon."

I murmured a soft thank you, but my throat was dry. His dark eyes held mine a moment longer, as if trying to see something deep within. Then he turned and left.

"Lightning, Olivia?" my uncle asked, eyes twinkling, questioning how I felt for the man.

My cheeks flushed and knew I could not hide any emotion from my uncle. "Lightning," I repeated.

"Not just for Rhys, either, hmm?" he queried, then chuckled when I blushed even more hotly.

Hmm, was right. I felt *something* for two men. What was wrong with me?

3

S IMON

"By the looks on your faces I missed something," I said to Cross and Rhys, pouring whiskey into three glasses. I picked up my own as I eyed them.

"Not something, some*one*," Cross replied, downing his shot in one big gulp.

"If it was Peters, I ken. The bastard said he wanted to finish the deal to get to the dance. I believe his words were, 'I've got a fancy piece I want to get my hands on. Her being prim and all, a dance is the only way the virgin bitch will let me touch her.'"

I tossed back my whiskey as I thought about the bastard's words. I didna like to hear a woman talked about in that way, no matter who she was. If I were her father or brother or any relation whatsoever, I would have beat him and left him for the vultures.

Rhys leaned back in his chair and crossed his arms over his chest. "He said that?"

I nodded, placed my forearms on the table. "If he didna have the stud horse we want, I wouldna get near the man."

"He was speaking of Olivia," Rhys shared.

"Olivia?" I asked, my voice loud, even over the tinny piano music. I glanced left and right at the others in the saloon, then leaned forward and lowered my voice. "Who the hell is Olivia?"

"She's the one," Cross said.

"He's right," Rhys added. "She's definitely the one."

I couldna help but look at them in surprise, for having both men agree on a woman had ne'er happened before.

"And Peters talked about her that way?" I asked. "What is the chance he will win her?"

"None," Cross replied.

Rhys looked between us, tilted his chair back on two legs. "Peters touched her," he said.

Cross placed his forearms on the table, too. "What?" he shouted. "How?"

"I don't know the details, but she had bruises on her wrist. Her uncle will keep him away from her now that he knows of what the bloody bastard's capable."

"That fucker's insane. From what I can tell of his character, he could inflict more than bruises." The idea didn't sit well and I hadna even laid eyes on the woman my friends were ready to claim.

Hell, we were more than friends. Rhys was a brother forged by battle, by hardship and life in a corrupt army regiment. We, along with the other men at Bridgewater, persevered and built the ranch on our own. Our safe haven, our land, our family. Together, Rhys, Cross and I would, someday, claim a woman as ours, just as we'd learned from our time spent defending diplomats in the small middle eastern country of Mohamir. Disappointed by the Victorian social values, we adopted the Mohamiran ways where a woman was bound to more than one man, possessing her and cherishing her. Multiple husbands were for the wife's own good, for she, and any children produced in the union, wouldna be without a man's protection.

Rhys and I met Cross when we arrived in America. He'd joined us in a fight to protect a whore against a group of men set on raping her. We'd left Boston together and he'd fled west with us. The journey and the years together since had forged a brotherhood just as readily as had the war. We helped build Bridgewater into the successful ranch it was with the other men and the three of us would claim a bride together.

Kane and Ian had married Emma the year before, Andrew and Robert had claimed Ann prior to that. Over the winter, Mason and Brody had found their bride, Laurel, when they rescued her from a blizzard. We hoped we'd find a woman of our own, but it wasna an easy task. To find a woman that one of us wanted was nae as hard, but finding one woman all three of us longed for was much more difficult.

This arrangement—three men for one bride—wasna something we shared with the world, so it was quite difficult to ken when a woman would want all three of us.

We'd share, we'd claim, we'd possess her together. We just didna ken who she was yet. It seemed, though, that both Rhys and Cross kent this woman Olivia might be the one. It boded well if both of them found her appealing.

"Describe her," I said.

Cross indicated with a tilt of his chin. "Hair as dark as yours."

"Petite," Rhys added, using his hands to indicate her height, then shifted his hands to show off the shape of her curves.

Cross laughed. "It is true, she has very nice curves."

"There are women upstairs with dark hair and curves," I

countered, referring to the loose women who worked above the saloon servicing patrons all night long.

Both men's faces hardened and I feared my nose would be broken if I spoke again of this Olivia woman in a disparaging way. "Shit," I muttered, then held up my hands to ward them off. "It's like that."

Both men nodded. "It's like that," Cross repeated.

"I met her uncle," Rhys said. "The name Weston mean anything?"

I thought about where I'd heard the name before, and then it came to me.

"The deal with the cattle?" I asked.

"Didn't Kane say that he...?" Cross asked, but cut off the end of his question, for we all kent the answer.

Both men grinned and I joined them, knowing that Olivia's uncle would approve of our ménage lifestyle, for he lived it himself. Kane had said the man who'd sold us the cattle the previous summer shared a wife with another man, but seemed to have kept that fact a secret from his niece. Kane had only said good things about him, so if he vouched for Allen Weston, then it was good enough for us. It only helped our cause when we wanted to marry her, for her uncle wouldna disparage three men claiming her. He'd see it as a perk.

I poured another round of whiskey. "She's ours."

OLIVIA

I couldn't sleep, too restless with the handsome faces of Mr. Cross and Mr. Rhys haunting me as I tossed and turned. I relived every moment of both dances, their words, the feel of their hands upon me, their distinct scents, Mr. Rhys' unusual accent. Everything. I groaned. Nothing would erase their images from my mind so I put on my robe and went to the kitchen for a snack.

"You were quite a catch at the dance," Uncle Allen said, surprising me as I came into the room. I should have seen him there, and it was clear indication my mind was wandering. He had a cup of coffee in hand, the steam rising from the top. How he could drink something so strong and fall asleep afterward was beyond me.

I went to the icebox and took out the pitcher of milk, poured myself a glass and joined him at the table. We took our meals in the kitchen, the two of us simple enough where we did not need to eat in the much larger dining room. While Uncle Allen was quite wealthy, he did not flaunt it and I'd grown up the same. The house wasn't large or ostentatious like others nearby where money was flaunted; it was just big enough for us to be content. We were both simple people with basic needs.

I could feel my cheeks heat and so I took my time drinking my milk to collect myself. "Yes," I replied neutrally.

"Two men especially were very handsome and seemed very taken with you."

Handsome? Mr. Cross and Mr. Rhys were not just handsome. They were stunning, virile, strong, intense. They were...lightning.

He had a hint of gray in his hair, but otherwise his age did not show. He was well connected in the Helena community and beyond through his work. The fact that he knew men from the Bridgewater Ranch was quite a coincidence, yet showed how powerful he was in the Territory. While he was busy with all of his endeavors, I wasn't as settled, perhaps because I'd been waiting for something more. Lightning. I'd been waiting for that.

I could not avoid looking at Uncle Allen any longer. He had

always been able to see all of my secrets, although I did not have many. "They are both very handsome, both very...manly," I replied, trying to be as neutral as possible.

He smiled. "They are that. I know some of the other men from Bridgewater quite well. I have nothing but good things to say and if you are amenable, if these men come calling, I will be more than happy to welcome them into our home."

"Them? I doubt one will come, let alone both of them."

"I believe Rhys said there's a third man from Bridgewater here in town as well. Simon McPherson."

A third. Could he possibly be as attractive as the other two?

"Nothing will come from meeting either man," I said, cutting off any hope he may have at making a match. "They are not from here and clearly spent the evening dancing with women to pass the time as they are here on business."

"I did not see either man dance with any other woman," he countered, picking up his coffee and taking a sip.

My heart leapt at that thought, but surely he was mistaken. I shook my head at the silly notion. "It matters not. They are most likely on their way back to Bridgewater as we speak."

"At this time of night?" He shook his head. "I will not force any man upon you, nor will I keep you from one who has captured your heart. As I said, you will know when the right man comes along."

I took a sip of my milk, and then said, "What if it feels right with more than one man?"

I winced, worrying my uncle would think me too forward.

"More than one man?" He considered, but did not seem stunned by my question. "You mean both Bridgewater men?"

I nodded.

"I am not averse to the notion of a woman having more than one man protect her. So, did the lightning strike twice, then?"

He grinned and I blushed.

"You don't think something's wrong with the feeling of lightning striking with two men?" Surely something was wrong with me if I did so, or I'd have to pick one and that would be quite hard.

"Olivia, I have something to tell you. You're well old enough now to know and, hopefully, to understand. I—"

The sound of broken glass followed by a loud crash cut off Uncle Allen's words.

He stood quickly, his chair scraping against the floor as he ran toward the front of the house. I followed along directly behind him.

I smelled smoke before I saw it and then there were the flames.

"Fire!"

4

𝓡 HYS

Pounding on my hotel room door woke me with a start. I shot up in bed, noticed it was still dark, and wiped my hand over my face. I hadn't fallen asleep readily; seeing Olivia's face in my mind and remembering the feel of her waist beneath my palm had made my cock rock hard. I hadn't been able to sleep with a bloody cock stand, so I'd made myself come to ease the ache, thinking of her as I did so. Only then, did I fall into a fitful sleep. Unfortunately, I was being roused when I had finally settled in.

"What?" I shouted, tossing my legs over the side of the bed. More pounding. I stood, went to the door and pulled it open, stark naked. Whoever wanted to disturb me in the middle of the night could get an eyeful for all I cared. "What?"

Simon and Cross were at the door, and from the sight of them in the dimly lit hallway, they had hastily dressed. "There's been a fire at the Weston house. Allen Weston sent for us."

I ran my hand over my face again, and then turned into my room to throw on my clothes.

"Bloody hell. Was anyone hurt? Olivia?"

Simon stepped into the room. "We dinna ken for sure, but we've been told they are both fine."

The thought of Olivia being hurt in a fire had me dressing with additional haste. I stood, skipping a tie or even doing up all of my buttons. Tucking my shirt in was wasted effort. "Let's go."

Even if Allen Weston hadn't provided the address, the residence was not hard to find, based on the strong smell of smoke and the number of people milling about at such an hour.

The sight of Olivia, wearing a white robe, her hair long and unbound down her back, had my heart skipping a beat. If she weren't standing in front of her house that had been, from the looks of it, only partially ruined, I'd be quite pleased by her less than modest appearance. But no maiden should be seen in such a way—nor a wife for that matter—by the general public, and the idea of any man seeing her thusly had me stripping off my shirt and giving it to her.

"Take this." Those were my first words to her. Not overly comforting or reassuring, but she needed to be covered. Now. "Please put this on over your robe."

She froze in place as I started to unbutton my shirt, ogling my chest as it was revealed. Probably not my wisest of decisions, but she needed to be covered more than me.

"No," Mr. Weston said, undoing the sash of his dark, long robe and taking it off. He wore pants and a dress shirt, although some of the buttons at the collar were undone. It was as if he hadn't fully undressed from after the dance. "This will be more appropriate for everyone."

Cross took the robe from the man and moved to stand behind Olivia to help her into it.

Simon introduced himself to both of them and shook Allen Weston's hand. "Are either of you hurt? Burned?" he asked, looking Olivia over. It was the first time he'd seen her, and his gaze was more clinical that sexual.

She shook her head and looked over her shoulder at Cross as she slipped her arms through the sleeves. "No, we were both awake and in the kitchen."

"It was a rock. Broke the window," Mr. Weston said, glancing over to his house and where the damage had been done. Besides some streaks of soot on his face, he seemed fine. Angry, but fine. "Then he tossed in a flaming whiskey bottle. The floor in the foyer is stone, but the liquid spread and caught the walls."

I glanced at the house. It was two-story and made of quarried stone. The front door stood open and the front windows on either side of it were broken. The fire did not appear to have spread much, most likely due to sturdy construction. While the house was not overly large, there was no question that we stood in a well-to-do neighborhood. It was much smaller than Mr. Weston's vast means, but he did not seem the type of man to flaunt his wealth. Unfortunately, that wealth was most likely the motive for the fire.

Neighbors—no doubt awakened by the commotion—were standing about in various states of dress, watching and speaking to each other in hushed voices.

"Ye said *he* as if ye ken the person," Simon said. His accent was pure Scot, but when he became angry, the burr was much thicker.

Mr. Weston nodded. "I can't say with complete certainty, but I think it was Clayton Peters."

Olivia held the front of the robe closed, her hands up by her neck as if she were chilled. It was a warm night, so I was worried about shock, but she seemed calm enough. I would watch her closely though and at the first sign of unease, we'd whisk her away.

Cross took hold of Olivia's hand and slid the overly long sleeve of the robe back to look for the bruises I'd mentioned. There, on her slim wrist, I could see them, mottled and dark, even in the night. Her hand was so small, her wrist so narrow and delicate in Cross' hold, he could easily snap her bones. She'd been lucky with Peters. When I got my hands on him, he'd know what it felt like to fight someone of his own size.

"Because of this?" Cross asked.

Olivia tugged at my friend's hold and he let her go, the long sleeve covering her hand once again. Clearly, she didn't want to be the reason for all of the destruction and Cross must have noticed it as well.

"This isn't your fault, love," Cross told her, carefully pulling her hair out from beneath the robe so it hung long down her back.

I was jealous of the man, for he knew what her hair felt like. I imagined it to be soft as silk.

"Oh, no, Olivia. This is Peters' doing. Not yours," her uncle said with certainty.

She nodded and stepped closer to her uncle. "If I hadn't made him angry, then—"

Mr. Weston shook his head. "No," he replied. "The only way to make him happy is if I hand over my money to him and that's not going to happen."

"He won't stop," she said, her eyes wide and wild.

With his hands on her shoulders, he looked at his niece. "No, I don't think he will. While this isn't your fault, I think it's more about you than me. He's angry at being rebuffed and he will, most likely, try something else."

I agreed with the older man.

"Then we must go away where he can't get us."

"I'm staying here, but you'll go."

She shook her head. "No, Uncle Allen, you can't. He's dangerous."

He cupped her jaw so she stilled her motion. "To me, he's not. He could, at a minimum, compromise you and then where would you be? Married to the damn bastard. I couldn't live if something like that happened."

Olivia pursed her lips for she knew the answer. So did the three of us. She would be married to the bastard, stuck with him for a lifetime of cruel treatment.

"If he resorted to setting fire to our house," he continued, "he could want to truly harm you."

"If he wants the money, he could...he could kill you to get it." Unshed tears filled her eyes, made them glisten in the moonlight.

"He won't get a dime, I promise."

I glanced at Simon, then at Cross. Both men nodded.

"She'll come with us back to Bridgewater. No harm will come to her," I said, vowing to protect her.

Mr. Weston looked at me over her shoulder, then at the other men. "Yes, Bridgewater is a safe place for you, Olivia."

"You want me to go off with three men? Three strangers?" She waved her hand in our direction.

"Their reputation precedes them. I know other men from their ranch and I'd trust them with my life. Yours, as well. They are honorable." He looked at me directly. "You have no idea how important she is to me."

"We will keep her safe," I vowed.

"Protected," Cross added.

A horse whinnied in the background, the fire brigade's pumper being pulled down the street and back to the station. With the fire out, there was not much more they could do.

"There is one stipulation." He took Olivia's shoulders and turned her to face us, her eyes wide, her body shrouded in the overly large robe. "You must marry her."

"What?" she cried, spinning back around, the robe swirling

about her legs. "Uncle Allen, perhaps *they* are doing this for the money!"

She didn't dare glance at us, for it was clear she knew the words were insulting. The barb did not hit its mark, for we all knew she was under duress.

"We don't need your money. Bridgewater is self-sufficient," I said.

"Yes, but marriage, that's not necessary—"

"Olivia. Stop." At her uncle's words, Olivia quieted, but I could tell she wished to argue. The tone of the man's voice was enough to keep her from brooking further argument. "Lightning, remember?"

She bit her plump lower lip and nodded, glancing at the three of us in turn. I had no idea to what her uncle was referring regarding lightning, but Olivia did.

"But...but how do I choose?" she asked, her voice low, but I heard it readily enough. So had the others. The fear for her safety lessened, knowing that this man was giving his niece to us. He, too, was honorable if he expected marriage before letting us take her. While we'd honor whatever gentlemanly rules existed when it came to being in the presence of a maiden, her virtue would still be in tatters upon her return regardless of our good behavior. Three bachelors didn't just take an unmarried woman to their ranch, no matter the reason.

In this instance, Mr. Weston could feel confident in her safety, Olivia would know our intentions were honorable and we'd know that she belonged to us. I could see his request for more than just honor. If something did happen to him, she'd inherit all of the Weston fortune. But married, it would pass to her husband, therefore preventing Peters from getting a dime. It was an uncle's way of protecting his niece and I had to respect him for that.

We should have run away at the idea of Mr. Weston forcing us to marry Olivia, but for the first time, she was the woman we wanted. I flicked my gaze to Simon, who'd had the least interaction with her, but he nodded his head, his intentions silent but very clear.

"Choose?" Weston asked. "You don't have to."

5

$\mathcal{O}$LIVIA

An hour later we were in the home of Uncle Allen's close friends Roger and Belinda Tannenbaum. If they were surprised to see us with three burly men in tow, they did not show it. When Uncle Allen announced I would wed all three of the men, they didn't blink an eye, which seemed quite odd. Was it because it was so late an hour and they were not fully awake? That was doubtful, since they sent one of their servants off to fetch the minister. It wasn't until then that I began to panic.

"I can't marry three men!" I cried, glancing between the formidable trio standing in the Tannenbaum's comfortable living room. "It isn't done."

"Actually, Olivia, it is," Uncle Allen replied.

I frowned, confused. Was I hearing him correctly? Had I hit my head in my rush to leave the burning house and I didn't remember?

He stood and went over to where the Tannenbaums sat across from us on a wide sofa and sat down with Belinda between the two men, placing his hand on top of hers in a surprising move. "This was what I wanted to tell you earlier before that damn rock was thrown." He took a deep breath, and then said, "Belinda is my wife, too."

He looked at the woman I'd known my whole life and gave her a sweet smile, then turned to me.

I stared at their joined hands, confused. "How can you be married to...to them? You live with me."

I could feel Mr. Rhys, Mr. Cross and Mr. McPherson watching the conversation unfold and they did not seem the least bit horrified by what my uncle was sharing. It was as if they already knew.

Nodding, Uncle Allen continued. "I do. When your parents died and you came to live with me, you were too young to understand the dynamic of two men claiming a bride and besides, the townspeople would not be forgiving. It was important to maintain appearances and give you a comfortable home, yet Roger and I, together, are married to Belinda. Those nights when I went out of town for business and Hattie stayed with you? Remember?"

It was as if a veil had been lifted off my face. "You came here, didn't you?"

"Yes. Do not be mad, or at least do not be mad at me just yet. Think on this for a little while. It's been a long night. These three men," he lifted his hand and indicated the men from Bridgewater, "will be your husbands. You felt a connection, what some call chemistry, with the two at the dance. It's all right to be enamored and attracted to more than one man, as Belinda can tell you. As I said, you don't have to choose one of them. You will have all three."

I glanced at the men. They were all so handsome, so big, so...breathtaking that the idea of belonging to all of them only made me panic more. I stood, shook my head and paced back and forth in front of the cold fireplace. "No, no, this is insane! I would have known, I would have—"

"Olivia," Belinda said, standing and coming before me. She was in her late forties with very pale hair, now pulled back in a simple braid for sleep. She'd donned a modest dress after our surprise arrival and I'd never seen her so simply put together. She took my hands in hers and gave them a squeeze. "I love them. I love them both. I *love* being married to both of them. Remember what your uncle always said about the man you are to marry? What I've always told you?"

She stood so close I could see the blueness of her eyes, the earnestness there. She'd always been kind to me, like a surrogate mother, involved in my life for as long as I could remember. Even as just a family friend, she'd answered all of my questions about becoming a woman. Even though Uncle Allen had been there for me regardless of my need, sometimes a girl needed a woman to confide in. She smiled softly. "What is it?" she prompted.

I pulled my hands free and wrapped them around my waist, as if I could keep myself from falling to pieces. "When I find the right man, it will feel like I've been struck by lightning." I sighed, then glanced over at the three men and I felt it again. They were not dressed as expected out in society, but none of us were. They wore no jackets, only their shirts and Cross' wasn't tucked in, Rhys' buttons weren't done up to his neck and Simon's sleeves were rolled up to show off tightly corded forearms dusted with dark hair. All were tall, serious and handsome. One fair and two dark haired men who intended to marry me. The idea was exhilarating and absolutely petrifying, as I'd never really felt the true interest of one man, let alone three, until now.

"I felt it when I met your uncle." Belinda's words had me turning back to her and I saw the love bright in her eyes, in the wide smile. "And again when I met Roger. I wanted them both and they wanted me."

"But it's so...wrong." I covered my face with my hands, and then pulled them away as I realized my blunder, tears sliding down my cheeks. "Oh, Belinda, I'm so sorry! I didn't mean your marriage was wrong—"

She held up her hands, a simple gold ring on her left ring finger and a similar one on her right. I had never known what the one on her right hand was for until now. She had one for each one of her husbands. "It's all right. This is overwhelming for you. Quite a terrible night, but look." She waved her hand toward the three Bridgewater men. "They are here for you."

"I...I don't even know them," I admitted.

I felt even worse now, for the men just looked at me with seriousness, yet a hint of concern shone in their eyes. While one I'd never even spoken with, the other two *had* been remarkably kind.

"How can you *give* me to strangers?" I asked Uncle Allen as I wiped the tears on my cheeks

"You said you felt a connection, a spark with them, that you were worried about being attracted to two men at the same time. Your head may be telling you it is wrong, but your heart will always tell the truth."

I chanced a glimpse at Mr. Rhys and Mr. Cross, one's eyebrows went up, the other smiled broadly.

"Is that true, love, that you are attracted to me and Cross?" Rhys asked. I noticed the term of endearment he used and it didn't feel dirty like it had when Mr. Peters had called me 'sweetheart.'

"It's all right," Melinda said, urging me to share my feelings.

Reassured by her smile, I nodded.

At that, the three men stepped forward. "May we have some

time alone with Olivia before the minister comes?" Cross asked Uncle Allen.

He gave his assent and stood. Melinda gave me a quick hug and left, holding hands with her two husbands. *Two husbands!*

I felt so incredibly uncomfortable standing alone in a room with three men, strangers, who were going to marry me. Not one, not two, but three! I couldn't look at them and had no idea what to say, so I kept my gaze firmly on the Oriental rug at my feet and my hands clenched together in front of me.

"Come here, Olivia," one of them murmured. I looked up and saw that it was Cross who had spoken. He sat down on the sofa where my uncle had been. "Please," he added.

His voice was calm, his eyes gentle. I glanced at the other two who gave slight nods of encouragement. I swallowed at the way they towered over me. I felt dwarfed beside them and should have cowered at their domineering presence, but instead it made me feel as if I was sheltered, that they blocked out the entire world; Mr. Peters, the fire, even Uncle Allen's surprising pronouncement.

I took the final step to Cross, but instead of sitting beside him, he took my hand and tugged me down onto his lap.

"Oh!" I cried at the feel of his hard thighs beneath my bottom. His arms came about me and pulled me in so I was sheltered, my cheek against his chest. I could hear the steady beat of his heart and his clean scent swirled around me. This was the first time I'd ever been held by a man and I felt the hot jolt once again. He was so warm and yet I shivered. It felt so wrong and so right at the same time.

"Mr. Cross, we shouldn't—"

"We should," he countered. "And my name is just Cross."

The other men came closer, Mr. Rhys sat next to us on the sofa and Mr. McPherson moved a desk chair and placed it directly before us. They surrounded me and there was no escape, however they still did not feel threatening and I truly did not wish to move.

"This lightning, explain," Mr. Rhys said.

His dark eyes watched me carefully.

"It's a feeling, when you meet the right person," I replied. "Uncle Allen wanted to ensure I didn't compromise on the man I was to marry."

"You felt it with me?" I could see the hope in his eyes. Was the feeling reciprocated?

I nodded.

"And with me?" Mr. Cross—Cross—asked. His chin rested lightly on top of my head.

Were they always this direct? Always so open about their feelings? Weren't men supposed to be the ones who never shared or showed any kind of emotion?

I scrunched up my face and squeezed my eyes shut, dreading voicing my own feelings aloud. "Yes," I exhaled quickly.

I didn't want to look at them, to see the horror or the amusement or the disgust on their faces at admitting my feelings for two men. Would they consider me loose and immoral?

"And what about me, lass? Think ye can feel something for me as well?" Mr. McPherson's words were thickly accented, so much so that the word *well* sounded more like *wheel.*

I peeked out from around Cross' arm to look at Mr. McPherson. Gone was the look of a harsh warrior, a man ready to conquer the world and slay dragons as necessary. Instead, it was a man with the corner of his mouth tipped up and question in his eyes. He was the biggest of the three men, with dark hair that was overly long, a square jaw and a blunt nose that had a crook in it. He was handsome in a rugged, brutish sort of way, but when he looked at me so endearingly, I could see he was gentle as well.

I could also discern the worry on his face, for it seemed these men did things together, including marriage, and if I did not like all of them, one would be lost, perhaps cast adrift and alone. Mr. McPherson had much riding on my answer. In that moment I realized perhaps I could hurt him more than someone as sinister as Mr. Peters.

"I cannot say, for I do not know you."

"Then we will change that," he murmured.

"You don't think there's something wrong with me then? I am not wanton," I stated baldly.

Simon's gaze lowered to my lips, then raked over my body. "Nay, lass, we dinna ken a thing wrong with ye."

Cross shifted me in his arms so that my head rested against his arm and he was looking down at me. "You can be wanton for us any time you wish," he offered, then said with more seriousness, "I felt it, too, Olivia, when we were dancing, and having you now in my arms...."

I saw something flare in his eyes, bright and hot, before he looked at my mouth. "I am going to kiss you."

He didn't give me time to think, or to refuse, or to even push myself from his arms before his mouth lowered to mine. His lips were warm and soft and gentle as they brushed over mine as if he were learning the curve of my lower lip, the corners of my mouth. All at once I felt hot all over and I was quite glad he held me so surely, for I would have slid off his lap and onto the floor otherwise.

To my surprise, my eyes had fallen shut and I had to open them to look up at him, at the first man to kiss me and saw him smile. "Again," he murmured, then kissed me once more, this time deeper, which elicited a surprised gasp from me and he used that to his advantage, his tongue slipping into my mouth.

His tongue!

The idea was stunning and yet this was most definitely what

wanton felt like. Tentatively, I touched mine to his and it was Cross' turn to groan. The sound had my heart pounding, had me feeling triumphant that I could actually please him with a simple kiss.

"Share," Rhys grumbled.

I felt Cross smile against my lips before he pulled back and propped me upright in his arms. "Ah, it seems I am not the only one who wishes to kiss you, love."

I knew my cheeks were bright red, for it was one thing for a woman to have her first kiss, it was another altogether to do it with two other men watching. So enraptured, I'd completely forgotten they were there.

Was I supposed to just get up and move on to the next man? It seemed awkward and very bold to do so. Before I could decide what I should do, Rhys pulled me out of Cross' arms and onto his own lap. He grinned down at me, the look wicked and friendly at the same time. "I've wanted to kiss you ever since I saw you at the dance."

I frowned. "I thought...I thought you were mad at me for questioning your honor."

"We have a higher standard to which you are accustomed, but no, I was not mad."

"Then you are willing to marry a woman just because you want to kiss her?"

He ran his knuckles over my cheek. "I want to do more than just kiss you."

I had a vague idea to what he referred and I was equally pleased and petrified.

"It's like you said, love. I just knew."

"Really?" I asked, surprised. He'd seemed so indifferent when the dance had ended. Then I remembered his vehement demand that I promise to seek his help if needed, and felt better.

He lowered his head and said, "Truly." I could feel the words against my lips then only the delectable pressure of his mouth on mine. Other than his lips on mine, the two kisses were completely different. Where Cross coaxed and played, Rhys delved and claimed. He angled his lips over mine and plunged his tongue into my mouth as if he needed me to breathe, as if he put his all into the kiss. My hands tangled in his hair, the feeling of silk slipping through my fingers. He tasted of peppermint, completely different than Cross. Even his scent was different. My skin tingled on my chin where his whiskers rasped.

"Does it feel as if we are strangers, love?" he asked, his nose brushing against mine.

I put my hands to my lips. They felt swollen and slick and hot.

"It feels as if you belong to me. To us. You are ours."

My body...it felt as if, as if...I couldn't explain it. I felt...hot and relaxed and tense and desperate and needy and confused and so many other things all at the same time. Beneath that, though, I felt...home. It was as if these men were familiar to me yet completely new all at the same time. It was quite strange and I did not readily understand, and as I felt prone to babble when nervous or overwhelmed, I decided it was best if I remained silent.

"Ye will have three husbands, lass, nae two." Simon murmured, the fiercest looking of the bunch, held out his hand in the space between us and sat patiently waiting. His dark pants were drawn tight over well muscled thighs and his shirt—snug over his broad shoulders—only defined how broad, how big, how, oh, enticing he was. He was letting me decide when, and if, I'd come to him next.

The room was quiet; only the ticking of a clock on the mantel and my soft panting breaths could be heard. Where my uncle and his...family went, I had no idea. I met Simon's dark eyes, searched for something, anything that indicated that he would treat me falsely, that he had less honor or integrity than the others.

I had to trust that these feelings I had were an accurate indicator of these men—*men*—being right for me. I'd waited for it all my life and now, once it happened, I was uncertain. I had to take a blind leap of faith, and Simon, Cross and Rhys were as well. They were sure, so very sure of this match and I was as much a stranger to them.

I climbed from Rhys' lap and placed my hand in Simon's. Placed my faith, my blind trust and hopefully my heart with him. With all three of them.

6

$\mathcal{S}$IMON

It was right then, when she looked at me with those ice blue eyes that held such nervousness, fear and hope that I kent Rhys and Cross were correct. She was the one for us. To say she was beautiful was an understatement. The dark hair and light eyes was a striking combination. While she was covered from neck to floor in her uncle's heavy and unflattering robe, I'd caught a quick glimpse of her in her own flimsy nightclothes and had seen her woman's shape. She was so small that I seemed a giant in comparison and I would feel terrible if I hurt her with even the gentlest of touches. How was she going to handle three men whose sexual needs were prolific enough where we would make almost constant use of her body? She would love it, we would ensure that, but just looking at her had a cock stand press painfully against my pants.

There was nae question to her virtue; the woman was a virgin and a very innocent one at that. I'd wager a bottle of the finest Scottish whiskey that she'd just had her verra first kiss, her first contact with a man. With men. Now I knew why my brothers— while our brotherhood was nae from blood, we were brothers nonetheless—were so adamant about her at the saloon. I would have reacted the same, ye ken. Nae harm would come to her again, nae while I was alive. And if I died protecting her, I would ken that Rhys and Cross would be there for her. That was the way in Mohamir and we respected the practice enough to want to live it ourselves. It had only been a dream, until now.

Now, Olivia's hand was in mine and I knew she was offering up more than just a simple touch. She was giving me things she didn't even know we would take. With that came trust and I wouldna do anything to tarnish that. Instead of setting her upon my lap as the other two had, I pulled her into the cradle of my legs so she stood directly before me, placing her hand on my chest. I wanted her at ease with me, a complete stranger.

As I held her gaze, my hands moved to her waist and they spanned her completely, my thumbs touching in the front, fingers at her spine. Her breath escaped in shallow pants and her eyes widened.

"Perhaps the order was a bit off, but since I'm to be yer husband, I should introduce myself. I'm Simon Angus McPherson of the clan McPherson, although these days I hale from Bridgewater. I may have been a wee lad in the Highlands, but I belong here, in the Territory."

I heard the knocker on the front door and Olivia's body tensed beneath my palms. "Nay, lass, tis only the minister."

She furrowed her brow. "You don't think I should be nervous of a minister at a time like this?"

I couldna help but grin at her sass. "Tis the man who avoids the parson's noose, nae the lady. Dinna worry, for the man will only change yer name, the rest," I paused and brushed her hair back from her face and then cupped my hand at her nape, "we will change as we go along. All four of us. Together."

She eyed me closely, as if testing the truth behind my words. "Surely the minister will not marry a woman to three men. The acceptance of such ways must only have a certain reach."

I offered one curt nod. "Aye." I glanced over her shoulder at Rhys and Cross, who sat casually upon the sofa, watchful yet alert at the same time. "Ye'll marry me to make it legal, but that is just paper, lass."

Voices came from the front entry and Olivia wanted to step away, so I let her.

"This is happening so quickly. It's overwhelming. All of it. I'm—"

I pulled her back into my hold, this time letting my hands roam up and down her back in a soothing way. "Ye are fine. Yer uncle is content as his only worry is for your safety and he's handed that protection to the three of us. Do ye ken we'll let anything happen to ye?" I gestured to Rhys and Cross as well as myself. "Ye are the center of our world now, ye ken."

The Tannenbaums came into the room along with the minister. Olivia stepped out of my hold and took a deep breath. The man of God was in his fifties and wore his white clerical collar along with his dark pants, white shirt and long robe. Obviously, he was awakened and brought from his bed with haste, but his smile was amiable for such a late hour. It was easy to forget everything when I had my hands on Olivia, but the reason for the swift nuptials was not going to go away when the sun rose. We needed to get Olivia out of Helena and away from the bloody bastard Peters.

"...so pleased you could come at such a late hour, especially after the dance. You remember my niece?" Weston spoke with the minister as he came into the room. We stood at their approach and Olivia was pulled into a discussion with the two about some charity luncheon that was to occur later in the month.

The Tannenbaums stood to the side but seemed not the least put out by the unusual evening, even with their wardrobe of nightclothes as a reminder. Perhaps it was that their secret was shed that had them at ease.

"I am quite pleased to be woken for a wedding. Most often it is because someone has passed on in the night, and it is such a sad affair. This reason, however, and for you, Olivia, is very good indeed. Now, then, which man is your lucky groom?"

"I am." I moved to stand beside Olivia, my hand on her shoulder, there for not only reassurance but also to prevent her from dashing off if she decided to change her mind. "Simon McPherson."

I shook the minister's hand as he looked me over. If he had concerns, he kept them to himself. Perhaps he knew Weston well enough to know he wouldna just marry his niece off to just anyone.

The minister cleared his throat with mild embarrassment. "Your uncle has given me a brief history as to what has happened this evening, therefore I will not need to ask the usual questions as to the reason for a hasty wedding."

Olivia's chin came up and I saw her cheeks flush a bright red. The color crept down her neck and beneath the robe and I had to wonder how far it traveled.

"Shall we begin, sir, for I would like to finally kiss her and I'd like to do it the verra first time with her as my bride."

The minister kept the ceremony blissfully short, only asking the most minimal of questions before pronouncing us husband and wife. Cross and Rhys had stood on my right while Weston stood beside Olivia, but I forgot all of them when I cupped her jaw and lowered my head to kiss her. This woman, she was my bride. She belonged to me in the eyes of God and her uncle and nae one could change that. The thought had pride filling me, and lust as well. Her lips were soft and tentative, yet when I lifted my head from the very brief, very chaste kiss, her eyes were blurry with awakened arousal and that pleased me verra greatly. The fact that I couldn't toss her over my shoulder and carry her to the nearest empty room so the three of us could have our way with her, only had my jaw hardening. Olivia's eyes widened at my change in demeanor, but I ran my thumb over her silky cheek in the hopes to soothe her, and ease my ache to touch.

Hearing Weston thank the minister had me breaking out of my reverie. I turned to the man and thanked him for his service and Roger Tannenbaum led him away, most likely allowing the man to finally get back to his bed.

"May we remain here until the morning instead of returning to the hotel?" Cross asked. 'I believe Olivia would be more comfortable doing so."

Melinda Tannenbaum smiled. "Of course. I've ordered a bath to be delivered to the blue guest room. Up the stairs and down the hall to the right. Olivia, you know where to go."

7

OLIVIA

Because I knew the house—I'd visited frequently all my life, and now I knew the true reason as to why—I led my husbands to the bedroom where they were going to take off my clothes and take my virginity. How *three* men did that I had no idea, but being the one to voluntarily guide them to my own deflowering made me very nervous. Nervous? No, that wasn't accurate. Petrified, embarrassed, worried. What if they found me lacking? What if I wasn't good at whatever I was supposed to do? How could I please them if I knew I wasn't good at...whatever? How did I make them happy when I had absolutely no idea—?

"Breathe, lass," Simon murmured, stopping before me as he passed through the door I'd opened. "'Tis nae a hanging."

While I knew he was trying to make light of the situation, it didn't help. In fact, it only had me bursting into tears.

I covered my face with my hands and couldn't stop crying.

I heard one of the men swear beneath his breath, the door closed quietly and then I was picked up in someone's arms and carried across the room. There, he sat and I was held, hands stroking over my body. The hands had to belong to more than one man, for I felt gentle touches on my legs, my side, even over my hair all the while being held tightly and securely within a snug embrace.

"Shh, it's all right, love, you've had quite a day." Rhys. I recognized his voice.

"Aye, verra brave." Simon's thick burr.

"You're safe with us. All will be better now." Cross. His words swiftly changed my emotion from sad and overwhelmed to anger. I lifted my head and turned toward his voice. I was held in Simon's arms with Cross and Rhys squatting before me. Concern was evident in their eyes, but I didn't care.

"I'm safe with you?" I lashed out, the three men my verbal victims. "I'm supposed to give myself to you, or you, or...or you and I have no idea what to do? How do I please *three* men? And better? How do you know things will be better? Someone set my house on fire and you think because we're married everything is better?"

Two sets of eyebrows went up before me, one dark, one light, surprised by my vehement tone and long windedness.

"Things will be better because you have us to protect you from the likes of Peters. In the morning, we will take you back to Bridgewater where you will be safe." Rhys' words were laced with absolute certainty. "It may not make the problem with the man go away, but it makes your involvement in it end. You do not need to worry any longer, as you need to let your uncle take care of Peters and we will give help to him if needed. I know he is a smart man, for he gave you to us, didn't he?"

I opened my mouth to speak but Cross put a finger over my lips. "How do you please three men? Trust me, love, you've already done that by marrying us. As to the rest, it is our job to teach you." He tapped my lips once then pulled his hand away.

"Ye can do nae wrong," Simon added, using his thumbs to wipe my tear stained cheeks.

His gentle actions wiped my ire away.

"I can do no right if I don't know what to do," I countered, sniffling.

"Are ye afraid?"

I sputtered. "How can I not be?"

The men looked at each other over my head and it seemed as if they spoke without saying a word.

"We will not take you tonight, Olivia, for you are tired and you will need your rest for what we have in mind," Cross told me. "Besides, it will be hard for you to keep quiet and I want privacy for when we take you."

"Why will I make noise?" While I tried to sound calm, I could hear the panic in my words. "You're not going to hurt me, are you?"

Rhys smiled. "No, we are going to do quite the opposite. It's going to feel so good that you won't help making noise."

"Ye are going to scream, lass," Simon finished.

I wasn't sure about that, but I did believe them when they said they wouldn't take my virginity tonight and was reassured and relaxed into Simon's arms.

"That doesn't mean we won't touch you," Cross added.

"What?" I asked, surprised. Simon lifted me with his hands about my waist to stand once again before him. With his hands on the sash of my uncle's robe, he pulled the bow loose. Hands at my shoulders slipped the garment down and off my arms and then off me entirely.

"You've had an overwhelming day and it's time for your men to take care of you. All you have to do, love, is feel," Rhys said, his voice low and gentle.

"It is our job to make you feel good. Let us show you how we can do that," Cross added.

"Trust us in this, lass," Simon added.

Their hands were on me, running over my shoulders through my robe and nightgown, down my arms, over my waist and hips, over the outside of my legs. Three sets of hands could cover quite a bit of my body at the same time. Their touches were all gentle, soft. Easy and relaxed. Soothing. Everywhere they caressed my skin tingled and came to life, even through the cotton of my nightclothes.

"Oh," I murmured, surprised by...by it all. "But...but I'm all smoky."

My eyes slipped closed of their own accord and I could easily do as they bid, for it felt so good. How they could set me at ease after a crying jag and a burst of anger was impressive and I had my first simple lesson; I should not underestimate them, for when they set about doing something, they seemed to do it quite well.

I didn't know how long I stood there as they touched me, but time had no meaning. I focused on the hard press of their palms, the curl of their fingers, the sound of their breathing, even the mingling of their scents.

Their touches had stayed to modest places, but every so often, a hand slipped below my hip to curve around my bottom or a thumb moved up to caress the underside of my breast. My eyes widened at the surprise of that, but the look on Simon's face when I did made me gasp. His eyes were so dark as to be black, his cheeks ruddy and he looked at me as if...as if he were a wolf and I was a very innocent little lamb. Perhaps that was true.

This time, when Simon's thumbs moved over my breasts, they didn't stop at the bottom curve but came up to brush over my nipples, which formed into tight little points. No doubt all three men could see them poking against the cotton of my robe. His large hands stilled, cupping my breasts as if he was feeling them, testing their weight, learning their curve.

"Simon," I breathed, holding his gaze as he began to gently knead my breasts, his fingers plucking at the tight tips.

I didn't remember it happening, but somehow my robe had come off and I stood before them in just my nightgown. Simon's hands were warm, even through the thin layer of fabric between my skin and his. From my periphery, I saw Cross lean in and kiss my neck, then work his way down to the juncture with my shoulder.

"Oh!" I gasped again. I had no idea my body could elicit such feelings, for as my nipples felt the hot sensation of Simon's playing fingers, somehow between my legs I felt swollen and aching and my core clenched in need. Yes, in need.

His lips worked the narrow strap along my shoulder to slip down my arm, the cool air in the room raising goose bumps on the exposed skin. Cross' mouth continued to lave my shoulder and neck as his hand slid over my hip. Rhys was not idle in all this, for as soon as my nightgown fell off one shoulder, he inched the second strap off my other shoulder as well, and the garment was held on my body solely by Simon's hands cupping my breasts.

I placed my hands on top of Simon's to keep him from letting the material fall, for I was naked beneath. He grinned.

"Like having your breasts played with?" he asked.

Cross and Rhys each brought a hand up and gently pulled mine away and back to my sides. While their holds weren't tight, they were insistent. Simon kept my gaze as he pulled his hands back and the nightgown slid to the floor at my feet with the slightest whisper of sound.

The men froze, their gazes riveted to my body for I knew they could see *everything*. With their hands back on my wrists, I felt gently powerless. I closed my eyes, blocking them out, but I could *feel* them looking at me.

Beautiful. Gorgeous. Perfect. Skin so pale I can see little veins like rivers. Coral, that's the color of her nipples, not pink. Nay, she's not pink there, but beneath that dark hair her pussy lips are.

With those last words, my eyes flew open and I tugged at my hands so I could cover myself. I wasn't exactly sure what a pussy was, but I had a strong suspicion.

"Nay, lass," Simon said with a slight shake of his head. "Dinna hide yourself."

"I'm...I'm embarrassed," I admitted. "I must smell strongly of fire."

"Yes, but we will bathe you. Later. First," Cross let go of my arm and undid the buttons on his shirt. "I will take my shirt off as well."

Rhys and Simon followed suit and soon enough they were all bare to the waist.

"I'm fully naked and you're not," I said, my gaze roving over the men's very solid chests. Simon had the most hair there, a mat of it soft and curly between his nipples that formed into a V to his navel, then into a narrow line that dipped beneath his pants. His belly was flat and muscles were visible beneath his tan skin. Rhys was the darkest of the three, his complexion more olive. He, too, had dark hair, but only a smattering on his chest and then nothing but well-defined muscles. Cross had no hair on his chest, only dusky flat nipples and never ending sleek skin.

I had no idea men looked that way without their shirts. Oh my. My fingers itched to reach out and feel how smooth their skin was, whether the hair there was soft, to touch all those hard muscles. These were not men who sat about idly; they worked and worked hard and it showed.

"Love," Rhys admitted, "the only way to keep us from claiming you tonight is for us to keep our pants on. I promise—"

"We all promise," Simon uttered.

"—that tomorrow when we are at home at Bridgewater, nothing will keep us from showing you our cocks, pleasuring you with them, making you ours."

"For now, though," Cross added. "We will please you."

I liked the idea of it, but the doing so was the confusing part. "How—"

I began to ask a question, but Simon leaned forward and took my now plump nipple into his mouth and my words ceased and a gasp escaped. Oh my! Simon's tongue flicked over the tip and I cried out. Men put their mouths there? It was so deliciously wrong, but I didn't want him to stop. Quite the contrary, I needed him to continue. Perhaps I voiced that thought aloud for his hand came up to cup my very lonely other breast and began to tweak and tug at the now distended tip.

That was just the beginning, it seemed, for I felt a hand slide down the bumps of my spine and over my bottom, curving around and back up again. Another hand smoothed over my belly and dipped lower to slip through the curls that covered my womanhood. For a brief moment, I clenched my hands and wanted to push the hands away, but then I didn't. I so didn't. For the light touch brushed over my heated flesh and I groaned, a deep body shuddering groan.

"That's the sweetest sound I ever heard," Rhys said, his voice deep and rough.

"She's so wet," Cross murmured. It was true, I was somehow slick down there and the way his finger moved I could hear it. It was another in a long line of actions I should feel mortified about but the way these men made my body come alive, I just couldn't. It felt...so good. I felt hot and pliant and I could barely breathe. Simon had switched to suckling at my other breast and I arched my back involuntarily for him to take more. I needed it...needed their touch...needed something but I didn't know exactly what.

A sheen of perspiration coated my skin and I felt my long hair cling to my back and nape. Cross' finger continued to slide over me, down the side of one slick petal to move it aside, then did the same with the other before finding my opening and circling, only the very tip of his finger slipping within.

"She's tight."

"Let me," Rhys said and I felt Cross' hand move away, which had a sob tear from my lips, only to be replaced by Rhys'. His touch was different. While he was just as gentle, he was more intent in his actions, his finger dipping in a touch further than Cross had, only to retreat and slide upwards to touch a place that—

"Yes!" I cried.

I felt Simon's chuckle against my breast.

"She tastes delicious."

I had no idea what Cross spoke about and I opened my eyes to see him sucking on his finger, the finger that he'd had between my legs.

"Wider, love," Rhys demanded, tapping me lightly on my inner thighs. I moved my right foot a little bit. "There, good girl."

"Now we can both touch you," Cross said, and I felt two hands between my legs, one running over the place, the amazing, incredible place that had me crying my pleasure aloud and the other dipping into my opening again and again, not far enough for my wants, but enough to make my body light up as if it were set aflame.

"Her clit's so hard, I bet she can come like this. Can't you, love, come for your men?"

I shook my head as I licked my lips, lost in the feel of their hands and I was thankful for their firm hold on the back of my thighs and at my waist. I didn't know what my clit was, but whatever they were doing I liked quite well. "I...I don't know what you mean," I practically sobbed.

"Do ye feel achy?" Simon breathed across the valley between my breasts.

"Hot all over?"

"Desperate?"

"Frantic?"

The men said word after word, all describing how I felt and I could only nod my head, my mouth open. I needed....

"We'll give it to you, love," Cross promised.

Their hands became even more attentive, Rhys' finger on that place that had me climbing higher and hotter and brighter, Simon's almost sharp nip at the tip of my nipple—

"Right...."

—and Rhys' finger that moved inside of me—

"...about...."

—only to slide back and touch me in the most dark and carnal of places.

"...now," Rhys vowed.

That slightest brush of his finger against my back entrance was what pushed me from the mountain I'd been climbing and I did a free fall, falling, falling with the most blissful pleasure coursing through my veins. White light shone behind my eyelids, my muscles tensed and a sob caught in my throat.

The men's hands continued to stroke and caress me until the pleasure ebbed and my body went limp. Simon sat back in his chair to keep his hands on me as Rhys and Cross moved to sit on the bed. I couldn't help the lazy smile that formed on my lips and I looked at each one of them with a blurry gaze.

"What was *that*?" I asked, my voice husky.

Simon's long fingers tightened about my waist. "*That* was yer men making ye come."

"Come?" I repeated.

In one motion, Simon stood and lifted me, carrying me to the copper bath and lowered me into the water, still warm.

"Pleasure. We gave you your pleasure," Cross clarified.

Simon grabbed the soap, rose scented, and began washing me with gentle efficiency, his soapy hands cleaning the stench of the fire from my body. I was lulled by the surprised bout of pleasure they wrung from my body so that I could no longer be embarrassed, even when he lifted me from the tub and dried me as if I was a child. The look in his eyes made it clear he did not think of me as such, then lifted me again to place me down in the center of the bed. It seemed the man enjoyed carrying me about. I felt the cool blanket against my overheated, sensitive skin.

"We gave you your pleasure, love," Cross repeated. "And we're going to do it again."

"And again," Rhys added.

"And again," Simon finished.

"But I'm not standing up," I said, coming up on my elbow.

While they smiled, they didn't laugh or make fun at my lack of knowledge in the ways of men and women.

"You don't have to be standing. Laying down works quite well, too," Rhys told me.

"I loved licking your taste off my finger. Your flavor is still strong on my tongue. I want more," Cross admitted. He stood and moved to the foot of the bed, placed one knee on the mattress and began to crawl toward me. At the same time, Rhys and Simon each took one of my legs in hand, spread it wide and held on.

Cross's green eyes were darker than I'd ever seen them, his cheeks and mouth flushed red, his hair rakishly falling over his forehead. His shoulders were so wide and yet his waist so narrow, and beneath his pants, there was a bulge a large—oh!

"More?" I began to pant in equal measures of anticipation and trepidation. "More what?"

"More *you*," he growled before he lowered himself between my thighs.

8

CROSS

"I don't know if I'll be able to sit on a horse," Simon grumbled as he ran his hand over his face, his whiskers rasping.

It was early, the sun barely up and we stood with our coffee on the back porch of the Tannenbaum house. We'd left Olivia sleeping, naked with the white sheet barely covering her lush body. Her hair was wild and tangled over the pillow, her lips were red and appeared bee stung from our kisses. But that hadn't been the only place we'd kissed. Simon and Rhys had spread her open for me and I'd eaten her pussy until she came. She was so sensitive, her clit a throbbing little bud, her arousal copious and her folds were delectable. Her taste, I couldn't get enough, but once I made her come, we traded places until we'd each had a taste of her and made her come. Her hot, sweet flavor was still on my tongue, even hours later.

While we all knew officially claiming her should occur only

once we were back at Bridgewater, it had been hard—no, practically impossible—not to want to pull my cock out and slide it into her slick, wet pussy. I'd been rock hard ever since I saw her at the dance and it wasn't going to go down any time soon. Even if I fucked her, I'd most likely want her again right away. I shifted myself in my pants and agreed with Simon's words. "I'm going to have to take care of the problem before we leave, but as soon as I see her I'll be hard again. Think we can make it home by nightfall?"

"Absolutely." Simon didn't waver in his answer. We *needed* to get home so we could take her. It would be a long night, but we would ensure Olivia enjoyed every minute of it.

Rhys joined us, his usually tidy appearance rumpled. "We need to get our woman out of here. Seeing her in that bed naked and sated has me wanting to fuck her, but we can't do it with her uncle in the house," he said, his voice grumpy.

"Tonight," I vowed.

"Tonight," Rhys agreed. Simon nodded.

Belinda joined us, and while clearly tired, was dressed immaculately. Her gaze was astute and she seemed the type of woman who missed nothing. "You gentleman are either not happy in the morning or are ready to depart. While the house is quite large, it is not as private as you would probably like." Yes, she missed nothing. She understood our predicament but was too much of a lady to say more.

"Yes, we are eager to get home," I agreed.

A small sly smile formed on her lips. "Yes, I'm sure you are. Would it be *easier* for you if I helped Olivia ready herself for the trip?"

Simon was the one who responded. "Thank you. I fear she is quite a temptation and we would be hard pressed to leave promptly otherwise."

She laughed at his words. "I'll have her ready in thirty minutes."

The Tannenbaum house was lavish enough to have its own stable and that was where Olivia found us within the half hour window. She wore what I could assume was one of Belinda's dresses, for her smoky robe and nightgown would not work for travel or anything else, really, for she would not be wearing a nightgown to bed ever again. The dress was forest green and cut well, but the color didn't flatter her as much as it would the older woman. I expected our bride to approach us with a sense of shyness after what we did with her only a few hours before or even a smiling, well satisfied glow about her, but I did not anticipate the fiery anger that shot from her eyes, the stiffness of her shoulders.

"You are done with me now?" she asked.

The sun was working its way up over the mountains in the distance and the air was warming. Only a few scattered clouds speckled the sky; it was going to be a pleasant ride. It was cooler in the stable, the scent of earth and horses strong. Both Rhys and Simon stopped what they were doing when we walked in.

"Done, lass?" Simon asked with an arched brow.

She stepped closer and I could see the bright flush to her cheeks as she placed her hands on her hips. "After...after last night you've had what you want?"

Rhys came up behind her and Simon and I came up beside her so she was flanked between us and one of the horses. "We gave you want you needed, yes," Rhys replied, although he was being neutral in his statement.

What was she angry about? We hadn't even seen her this morning.

"What I needed? I needed to be reassured by my husbands, not left in the hands of Belinda. What did you think I would feel, being abandoned and then told I had to dress to leave? Is this how you plan to treat me, for I will just stay here if you are."

My jaw clenched tightly as I crooked my finger, beckoning her closer without words. She swallowed deeply, but kept her chin raised as she closed the distance, close enough so I took her small hand in mine. With my other, I undid the placket of my pants and pulled out my cock. My rock hard, eager cock.

She gasped and tugged at my hold.

"You're an innocent and do not understand why we did not join you earlier in the guest room." I gripped the base of my cock and hissed, my cock pulsing with eagerness, pointing directly at Olivia. "We should have explained, and for that we are sorry, but did not want to frighten you, but there is no way around it. See my cock, love? It's hard, hard for you. See that fluid on the tip, it's all but weeping to be inside you."

When I began stroking from base to tip and back, she watched my motions carefully, and then glanced up at me through her dark lashes. There I saw curiosity and surprise and a hint of arousal. I wondered if she was wet beneath the long hem of her dress.

"I want to fuck you, Olivia, and if I had come to you this morning, I would not have been able to stop myself."

"Oh," she whispered, her eyes lowered once again to watch my hand.

My hips bucked involuntarily at the thought of her on her knees before me, her mouth a perfect O around my cock.

"We all want you, lass," Simon added. Perhaps she forgot the others were there, for she startled and turned her head to look at the front of his pants. I could see the clear outline of Simon's hard cock and I knew Olivia could as well.

"We want you too much," Rhys added.

Moving my hand, I took hers and wrapped it around my cock, placing mine on top and then started to move. I couldn't help the groan that escaped at the feel of her palm, her small fingers touching me, sliding up and down my length.

As I showed her how I liked it, I gave her a brief lesson. "My cock's going to fill your pussy all the way up, but for now, you're going to make me come with your hand. Remember last night when you came? That's how you're going to make me feel. This ridge, yes," I hissed as she slid a finger along the sensitive edge of the head. "It's going to rub over all the special places deep inside you and you're going to come again all over my cock. When a man comes, his pleasure erupts and his seed will ultimately fill your belly."

Simon and Rhys stepped close and began touching Olivia. Rhys grabbed a hold of her long dress and slid the fabric up her thigh, higher and higher until he could reach underneath, Simon doing the same on the other side. Soon, her dress was up about her waist in front and Simon tugged at the ribbon of her drawers, letting them drop to the ground. Simon started to play with her pussy from the front, Rhys reaching around from behind.

She stiffened as they began stroking her, but I continued to move her hand over my cock, my desire building at the base of my spine like a ball of fire, getting ready to explode.

"Someone may come in," she replied, skittish feelings fighting with her arousal.

"Nay, lass, we are alone," Simon said. "Ye are so wet, dripping on my fingers."

"Perfect," Rhys added and then her hand gripped my cock tightly as, I assumed, Rhys' finger found her ass and began playing.

"You shouldn't touch me there," she said, trying to squirm away, but she was held fast.

Sweat coated my brow, as I was more than ready to come, seeing Simon's hand glistening with her arousal and knowing

Rhys was beginning to play with her ass. I shifted my body to the side so that with the next vigorous stroke of her hand, I came.

I groaned and pulsed my hips as rope after thick rope of my seed shot onto the hay and dirt at our feet.

"Oh," Olivia said in surprise. My eyes fell shut as I savored the intense feeling, knowing I'd taught her how to work a cock. I released her hand, my cock too sensitive now for her to touch it. I sighed loudly, and then grinned, for I couldn't help it. The desperate ache had been relieved, if only temporarily. As for the others, they'd have their turn next. I moved to the side and the men walked her forward so I could place her hands on a hitching rail used while grooming a horse. "Put your hand here, love," I directed. Once she did so, Rhys pulled her hips back slightly and I knelt down before her, Simon at her side.

"What are you doing?" she asked.

"Playing," I said. "I'm going to play with your pussy and Rhys is going to play with your ass. We're going to make you come while you stroke Simon's cock next."

I took the hem of her dress from Simon as the man undid his pants and pulled his cock free, ready for her to practice her hand skills on another cock. It was Simon's turn to direct her, as I was more than content to play with her pretty pink pussy and stroke her to pleasure.

"My...I don't think you're supposed to be playing with my *ass*." She whispered the last word as if it were a dirty word.

"No, love, we will almost always play with your arse when we are with you, for soon you will take all three of us at the same time. One of our cocks will be in that sweet mouth, another in your perfect pink pussy, and the last in this tight, hot arse. Don't panic, we have to take your maidenhead first, but your pretty arse needs to be trained to take a cock."

I was flicking my tongue over her distended clit as my fingers held her open, but when she stiffened against my mouth and groaned, I had to assume Rhys had slipped a slick finger into her arse. I loved the taste of her on my tongue; the scent of her was sweet and so heady my cock was getting hard again.

"She's verra good with her hand," Simon commented, his voice deep and guttural. "I'm nae gonna last, lass, so finish me." I heard him shift, then grunt a hand slapping against the wooden wall to hold himself up.

"I've got one finger in her and she's so tight. I think, Cross, every time you flick her clit she clenches her arse nice and tight. When we get our cocks in here it's going to feel like pure heaven."

"It...it's too much," she gasped.

"My finger? It's just the beginning. Relax, that's it. It's my turn to come, love, but Simon's going to take my place."

"Oh," she gasped as the men switched places.

"I need a little honey from the honey pot, lass," Simon told her and I saw his finger dip into her pussy and come out dripping wet before moving over the tiny rosebud.

"Give me your hand, love, and show me what you've learned. I bet you can do it without me helping. Ah, yes," Rhys hissed. I glanced to my left and saw that Olivia was stroking Rhys' cock all on her own, one of his hands on the wall to keep himself upright, the other clenched in a tight fist at his side.

"Such a perfect, tight arse, lass. I'm going to start pushing in now, just like Rhys did."

She whimpered, but knew that for Simon's large size, he would be gentle with her. The pain and pleasure mix of ass play had me sucking on Olivia's clit with more vigor and dipping a finger into her pussy. After last night, I had a good idea of how to get her to come and I wanted to do that while Simon's finger was in her ass. I only wanted ass play to be associated with pleasure, right from the very first breaching.

"Cross is going to make ye come, lass. Take a deep breath now, and let it out. Such a good lass," he soothed as she groaned, a mixture of new feelings, being filled in the ass and pleasure of having her clit and pussy worked. "Be verra quiet so no one hears ye being pleased by your men."

When the fingers of her free hand tangled in my hair I knew she was about to come. I could feel her inner walls clenching down on the tip of my finger.

"Now, lass. Come for us now."

She did, right on command, her body dripping its pleasure onto my fingers as she bit her lip to stifle her cry, her body convulsing with her release.

"She's gripping my cock so tightly," Rhys said just before he groaned and I knew he'd found his pleasure as well.

I sat back on my haunches and wiped the back of my hand over my mouth as I looked up at Olivia. Her eyes were closed, her skin flushed, her mouth open and breathing heavily. Simon was still gently moving his finger within her ass until the last bits of her pleasure waned. When she opened her eyes, he stepped away and her dress fell back to the floor.

"That's why we didn't come to you, but instead of just playing, we would have taken you, taken your virginity, and when we do, we don't plan to let you up," I told her. Her pale eyes looked down at me, foggy with her arousal and quite pleased with herself.

"For days," Rhys added as he buttoned up his pants.

9

𝒪LIVIA

On our ride to the Bridgewater ranch, I didn't raise the topic of my angry outburst from the morning, for if I did, they might want to talk about the things we did directly *after*. While I now understood their reasons for leaving me alone in the guest room, I hadn't at the time. Fortunately, their tempers were such that they took the reasoning for my ire into account and hadn't yelled or even argued.

Twenty minutes alone in the stable with the trio had me learning there was more to having them take my virginity than I first imagined. It wasn't fumbling beneath the sheets in the dark.

When, to my complete surprise, Cross had opened up the front of his pants and pulled his...his cock out, I had no idea one could be so large. I assumed they were much smaller, for the idea of him fitting within me was preposterous. Then I saw Cross' cock and it was even thicker and at that point, besides being pleasantly distracted, I didn't want to consider it, or the size of Rhys' even further. They'd said they'd wait until we were at the ranch to do more—more of exactly what I couldn't be sure—so I had a reprieve until then.

Reprieve or not, that hadn't kept them from putting their fingers in my bottom, at least only two of them did, and that had been enough. I'd had no idea that was something done between married people; no whispering I'd heard by the younger married ladies had ever mentioned such attentions. It had felt...odd, and when Rhys had first pushed into me, it had burned a bit. But when he began moving very slowly in and out, like Cross' finger had been in my woman's core, it had been completely different. The intensity of the feelings—the *pleasure* there—was absolutely overwhelming. When Cross had licked me on that special spot between my legs, I'd come and come hard. It was as if each time they took me over that brink it was better and better.

I knew men felt pleasure as well, for why else would there be brothels in every town, sometimes more than one? The look on their each of their faces as they came was...powerful, for I knew my hand sliding up and down each of their thick shafts had been what did it. I'd caught on quickly after Cross had showed me how, and the smooth, hot, hard feel of each of them was impressive. Unfortunately, none of the men gave me much time to focus on them, for they'd very thoroughly taken care of me. When it was three against one, I was always going to be overwhelmed.

For the duration of the ride to Bridgewater I sat on one man's lap, then another, as it seemed they wished to take turns holding me. I was too sated from their attentions to truly argue, and perhaps this had been their strategy – to pleasure me so I wouldn't argue. I didn't comment on being shared, as I was quickly learning they were very possessive men and while they worked together as a team, they were individuals and needed their own time with me.

"Is that the stud horse you spoke about at the dance?" I asked, looking at the animal that was being led behind us. After our last break, Cross had climbed onto his animal and took my hand and lifted me up onto his lap. "Why can't I ride him?"

"It is, but while broken, he's new to us and we don't want to risk anyone getting hurt. Don't you like riding with your men?" he asked, running his chin over the top of my head.

I did, actually, enjoy being held. "It is new to me to sit with a man. Well, to do anything really with a man. Not only is it unseemly to do so before now, I was quite independent." The past tense disturbed me, for now that I was married, would I have the same liberties as I had when I lived with my uncle? I hadn't gallivanted all over Helena as my days were structured with social and charitable functions as well as playing hostess for my uncle—

"Oh," I said.

"What is it?" he asked.

"I just realized that my uncle did so much...presentation to keep me from knowing about his relationship with the Tannenbaums."

"How so?"

The horse's plodding gait had me shifting into Cross' body. While I wore a bonnet on my head, his large body shielded me quite well from the sun.

"He had dinner parties and could have done it with Belinda as hostess in my stead. He kept his house just for me. We didn't sit with the Tannenbaums at church and I know Uncle Allen didn't see them all the time, probably not as frequently as he'd liked. He sacrificed so much for me."

I felt Cross shake his head. "He didn't do it only for you. Do you think your friends and the other church members would approve of him sharing a wife with Roger?"

"No. Am I going to live solely with Simon then to keep up appearances?"

"Nay, lass," Simon said, bringing his horse up so he rode alongside us on one side, Rhys moved into position on the other. "At Bridgewater having several men care for one wife is the norm."

I glanced at him, so dark and handsome, his whiskers coming in quickly and black hair now covered his jaw. His hat was low on his head and he rode a horse easily. While he was at ease, I could see his eyes scan the horizon for any hidden threats. Rhys seemed to be the one who was studious and bookish. Cross was more lighthearted, while Simon was the serious one, although the attraction was not any less for it, the intensity of his gaze upon me just as hot.

He seemed to be the one who was the most protective, perhaps even possessive. We'd left Helena without incident but they had wanted to keep watch for Peters or any man he might have sent. So far, nothing.

"I've never heard of several men marrying one woman and I have to admit, am not used to the idea."

"You wouldn't be used to the idea of wedding just one man as quickly as you did either," Rhys added. "It was done with extreme haste."

True, it would have been a surprise even then.

"Simon and I were in the same army regiment. We left England and were stationed in the tiny country of Mohamir."

"Isn't that near the Ottoman Empire?"

Rhys smiled. "You know your geography. It is that country's custom for a woman to be married to more than one man, in some cases brothers, in others, men who have come together and vowed to treasure and protect one woman."

"In England, lass," Simon swore, "those bloody Brits often

marry for social standing or money and the men have strict rules for their wives, but none for themselves."

"There have to be some who marry for love," I countered.

"Aye, lass, that is true, but in the circles I traveled, it wasna the norm. We had friends whose wives were neglected and unhappy while they were off slumming in brothels. It disgusted us as to the lack of honor. In Mohamir, however, that honor existed and it was the way we want to be."

"Don't you and Rhys someday want women for your yourselves?" I asked Cross.

I didn't like the possibility of being left for someone else, for they were handsome men and surely women had flocked to them in the past. How could they not be sought after in the future as well?

"No, love. We only want you."

"We will always want just you," Rhys added. He angled his head and looked at me with dark intensity. "You may not think it now, but the Mohamiran way protects the wife, for if something were to happen to one of us, you would still have the others to cherish you - you and children that will surely come. You will never need of anything ever again."

"If you liked their ways so much, why didn't you stay there?"

"Our commander did something...terrible and one of our friends, Ian, was framed for the crime. We knew he was innocent and justice would not be served, so we left," Rhys explained. "As a group, we chose to band together and make a new life. We traveled to America to find a place where we could practice what we learned in Mohamir, while escaping Evans and any repercussions that might follow us."

I turned my head so I could look up at Cross. His eyes were so green in comparison to Rhys and Simon's dark ones. "What about you? You sound as American as me. Surely you didn't spend time in Mohamir."

He kissed the tip of my nose. "I was raised in Boston and that was where their ship came in. I wasn't as big back then as I am now, but I was involved in a fight to protect a woman and these two helped me."

"There's more to the story than that, isn't there?"

Cross put his chin on top of my head once again, forcing me to not look at him anymore. "My past isn't a good story, love." His voice sounded flat at the mention of his childhood. "Bridgewater is my home now. Your home. It is where our future is. *You* are our future."

$\mathcal{R}$ HYS

"You went to Helena for a stud horse and came back with a bride as well?" Kane asked, holding the halter as Simon brushed the animal down. He'd been working in the stable when we arrived and had come to help with our horses.

"Turns out the man who sold us the horse is a bloody bastard and hurt Olivia and most likely set fire to her house." Cross shared the events of our trip with our friend.

"So you married her for protection alone?"

"We wanted her the first time we saw her," I stated plainly. "I knew when I danced with her, had my hands on her. There wasn't any decision to make "

Kane nodded. He was as dark as I, although a few inches taller. He'd married Emma the previous summer, saving her from a ridiculous brothel marriage auction. At the time I hadn't exactly understood the depth of his awareness that Emma was the woman for him and for Ian. They'd had only a minute or two to look at her before the auction had begun, but they'd known. Just like Cross and I had known at the dance.

He and Ian had protected Emma from the other men at the auction, but they'd married her because they wanted her. There was no doubt of the love match. They were very attentive to her, and she'd given birth to their first child not long ago.

Kane smiled and nodded. "Once the women hear of her existence, they will want to meet her straight away."

"Tomorrow," I said.

Cross shook his head. "Two days. We have yet to fuck her."

"And yet you are here talking with me?" Kane asked, head cocked in surprise.

"Simon remains at the house with her." After her enlightening outburst this morning, we agreed one of us would stay near until she became comfortable with us. "She's taking a bath. We gave her one hour of peace before we descend." Anticipation laced my every word.

"Go," Kane said. "See to your wife. I'll have the others help get the animals settled. I give you three days, consider the extra day a wedding present, and then we meet her."

Ten minutes later we entered through the kitchen door. Simon was sitting at the table reading a book.

He put it down on the table. "I have nae read one word as I ken she's up there," he pointed up at the ceiling, "naked and in a bathtub. After helping her with one last night, tis bloody impossible to sit here and give her some time."

"We're done giving her time," I said, turning toward the hallway.

Simon stood, the chair legs sliding loudly across the floor. "About damn time," he grumbled.

It was time to make Olivia ours.

We found her not in the washroom, but in Simon's bedroom, a bath sheet wrapped around her damp, naked body. I almost came in my pants just looking at her. I tossed the bag of my handcrafted dildos and plugs onto the bed for later and closed the distance between us. We'd surprised her, even though we'd clamored up the stairs and down the hall.

"You have a lovely home," she said, glancing around the room. We'd built the house with large bedrooms, for we were large men, and we'd hoped to someday have a wife who would spend the night in each of our rooms in turn. We also had extra bedrooms built with the hopes of children. Perhaps that day would come soon, for if we were skilled enough and the timing right, it could be in nine months or so. The idea of filling Olivia's womb with our seed and having it take root, to watch her belly swell with our child made my cock press painfully against my pants. If she looked, she wouldn't be able to miss it.

I chuckled at how she was trying to make small talk with just a scrap of white cotton covering her. She knew what was coming, for we'd clearly stated we would wait until we took her, and she was nervous. I didn't blame her. Three randy, eager men were going to strip her bare and take her virginity. Because of this, I took a deep breath and tried to will my cock down.

"Nervous?" I asked.

She gave me a tremulous smile. "You are very daunting." Her pale gaze shifted over each of us and widened as she watched Simon undo the buttons of his shirt.

"Nay, lass. We are three men who want to please our wife, to make her ours." He tossed his shirt onto the bed and then began to toe off his boots. I was undoing my own shirt when he spoke again. "We willna hurt ye. Ever. Now drop the covering so we can see ye."

Biting her lip, she considered, then dropped the sheet, letting it swirl to the floor at her feet.

I hissed out a breath at the sight of her creamy skin, her high, pert breasts, the dark thatch of hair at the juncture of her thighs. Her legs were long and she had dainty feet and her hair was pulled back into a ribbon at her nape.

The other men were almost as completely bare while I was still dressed so I, too, stripped. Clothing wasn't necessary for what we were going to do...for the next three days.

"Her pussy needs a shave," Cross commented.

Simon nodded his head. "Aye."

They stood eyeing her, Simon's arms over his broad chest. Their cocks curved up toward their navels.

One of Olivia's small hands moved to cover her pussy. "What? Shave my...my...why?"

"Did you like how we licked and sucked and ate at your pussy last night?" Cross asked, stepping closer. She retreated and the back of her legs bumped into the bed. "The way I did this morning?"

"Dinna lie, for we ken the truth. Ye loved it...three times," Simon said, walking around to the far side of the bed, placing a knee upon it and coming to kneel behind her.

She glanced over her shoulder, then at me and Cross. "Yes, all right, I did. I liked it very much."

Her eyes kept moving, looking us over one at a time, curious and nervous.

"This is your first time seeing a naked man, love?" I asked, brushing a dark curl behind her ear.

"Yes."

"Have a look at Cross while I go get the supplies for your shave. Simon will get you in position."

As I walked down the hall, I heard Cross' voice. "When you're pussy's all bare, the feelings will be more intense. Besides, we want to be able to see all your pretty pink flesh."

I grabbed the soap cup and brush and a washcloth and stopped in the doorway. Simon sat on the bed with Olivia's back at his front, her legs bent and spread wide at the edge of the bed, her pussy on perfect display. Cross had pulled a chair up from the corner of the room and sat directly in front of her.

I offered the supplies to Cross and he quickly settled into his task.

"But I don't want it bare," she replied, trying to squirm. Simon had his hands beneath her knees holding her still. No amount of effort on her part would have her moving.

"*We* want you bare so bare you will be."

Cross paused in his work and with his free hand, slipped a finger down the length of her folds, then slipped it inside. "This is our pussy, Olivia. Ours. Soon enough you will not doubt that."

A slippery wet sound filled the air as he pulled his finger free and returned to his task. She whimpered and we all knew she was not under much duress.

I moved onto the bed and positioned myself so I could play with her breasts. The flesh was so soft and plush, firm yet supply and pliant. The pale nipples tightened before our eyes and she gasped as I tweaked one, then the other.

"Like that?" I asked, her pale eyes shifting to me.

Cross slid the razor lower over her delicate skin and the patch of bare skin grew.

"Rhys," she murmured.

"What, love? Yes, you like it?"

She nodded her head against Simon's chest.

"How about now?" Did she like a little pain with her pleasure when I tugged on the tip, then pinched it? Did she like it soothing and gentle when I took the worked flesh into my mouth and licked over it and suckled? I felt her hands tangle in my hair as I closed my lips around one nipple and worked the other with my fingers.

"She dripping," Cross said, wiping the clean towel over her now smooth flesh.

"Get my bag," I told him as I saw her bare pussy for the first time. Her lips there were dainty and a lush pink, glistening with her arousal.

Reaching on the other side of her, Cross brought the bag onto his lap and pulled out the items I'd made. Winter was long in the Montana Territory and without a woman to keep us warm, I'd discovered that woodworking was a hobby at which I was quite good. I worked many things on the lathe for my friends' use on their wives. Dildos and butt plugs of various shapes and sizes, often made to specification. I'd made some for our future bride so we could play with her, however none had been used until now.

"What are those for?" Olivia asked, crinkle forming in her brow. Simon had not released her legs, which was good, for she was in the perfect position. Cross held up a thin, long dildo for me to see and I nodded.

"Here. Take it," Cross told her as he held it up.

Olivia took the wooden object and inspected it. It was dark wood, very smooth and very narrow, only as wide as my smallest finger, much smaller than any of our cocks. I'd made it just for this specific occasion, for her to take her own maidenhead as we watched. None of us wished to cause her pain and once she broke through with the dildo, we could take her without any fear on her part. Only pleasure.

Cross placed his palm on her lower belly and placed his thumb directly over her pink pearl. We could all see it clearly now and Olivia cried out at his touch. Her hand gripped the dildo tightly so her fingers turned white.

"I've made many things to pleasure you with. Right now, you're going to fuck yourself with the dildo, love, and break through your maidenhead."

"But...oh God," she moaned, Simon doing an amazing job of building her arousal, however she was quite sensitive and very responsive. I began to play with her breasts again, for I wanted her to be completely brainless and only feel. I wanted her to *want* to fuck herself. "I thought, I thought one of you would do that."

"We will, soon," Simon growled, barely holding on to his willpower. Just looking down the length of her body—parted lips, long neck, pert breasts with furled tips, lush belly and hips, smooth and bare pussy, then Cross' thumb working her slippery clit. She was all I'd dreamed of and more. There was just one tiny barrier still in the way.

"It's going to slide in so easily," I murmured. "Once that barrier is gone, we're going to fuck you. One at a time."

"I'm first, lass, and I canna wait. Can ye feel my cock at yer back?"

Simon took her hand and adjusted her grip on the dildo so she held it like a small spear and lined it up with her slick pussy.

"Will it hurt?" she asked me, her head tilted to the side, her pale eyes filled with trepidation. Cross worked her clit and her eyes slipped closed. I kissed her lips, for how could I not, then whispered, "If it does, it will only be for a brief moment. We will be watching, love, watching you ready yourself for us. It is going to be so beautiful to see."

"Now, lass."

11

OLIVIA

I was so overwhelmed! For a few minutes in my bath, I'd had private time to think about what was to come with the men, with their taking my virginity, and then they'd all but stomped up the steps, stripped off their clothes and beat their chests like cavemen. I had hoped for a husband who would dote and offer me attention and affection, and Cross, Simon and Rhys certainly did all of that. Their fervent attentions would be something to which I would have to accustom.

They wanted me! Even a very innocent virgin like me couldn't miss that fact. While I'd had my hand on their cocks earlier, seeing them naked and fully aroused was something else. Seeing one virile, well-formed man with a cock that was big enough to curve up and practically touch his navel was impressive, but I had three. Three! Three men and three cocks.

Simon was solid and broad and big and very, very large.

Everywhere. His cock was a ruddy red, the head flared and almost angry looking. Rhys, equally dark, was leaner, taller and his cock seemed longer, which should have been impossible because I didn't think Simon was remotely small. Cross, with his light hair and fairer skin, had hard, sleek muscles and a pale nest of hair at the base of his cock that made him so very different from the other two. That was just their bodies. The looks on their faces were almost predatory, as if they intended to circle me, stalk me, then take me.

The way my body heated at the idea, the way my nipples pebbled at the thought; I wanted it. I wanted *them*.

I was also...scared.

I'd forgotten all about being scared when Simon had held my legs open so they could shave me. If their goal was to keep me off kilter, then it was working, for I had never imagined such a thing, but Rhys' words and then his hands on my breasts had distracted me. *Everything* they did was a distraction!

Once finished, Cross began touching me with just his thumb and in a very specific spot. Circling and circling he worked that bundle of nerves that spread pleasure to my fingers, my toes, to my nipples, to every part of my body. Even then, looking down at Cross's cock, rigid and long between his legs, I'd thought he'd lean forward and push it in, but instead they'd pulled out this slim wooden contraption—a dildo, they called it—for me to break through my maidenhead.

My inner walls clenched as they gave me the directions, and again when Cross guided my hand and this wooden phallus to my opening. My newly shaved skin there felt cool, slick and very, very bare. I watched the dildo disappear, little by little as it began to fill me. My body clamped down on it, but it wasn't big like the men's cocks and I was frustrated. When I was able to slide it in so easily and so far, I knew something was wrong. I'd heard about pain during the first time, of some membrane inside ripping and bleeding. A man expected their bride to be a virgin and this barrier was the true sign, the official notice that she was pure.

My eyes widened in surprise when the side of my hand bumped my newly bare skin.

"It...it didn't hurt."

There was something wrong with me and they'd think I was a whore!

I let go of the dildo's small handle and grabbed Cross' forearms. I had to make him understand, for he could clearly see from his vantage point what was happening.

"I'm a virgin, truly." I tried to sit up, but Simon's hold on my legs prevented it. Slowly, Cross eased the dildo out and I gasped at the feel of the hard wood brushing against my inner walls. He held it up, coated in my glistening arousal, but no virgin's blood.

"Cross, please, you have to believe me!" I cried. I tugged at Simon's hold on my legs and he released me and I scrambled to sit up. There was nothing with which to cover myself and I could not escape the dominating presence of three large, aroused men. I couldn't discern from their faces what they were feeling. Did they think I'd tricked them? Tears welled—I couldn't stop them—and slipped down my cheeks.

Simon took hold of my arm and pulled me into him, his skin so warm and I could feel his cock prodding my belly.

"We believe you, lass," he said, wiping my tears away with his thumbs.

I frowned. "How? Isn't there supposed to be blood?"

Rhys shrugged, but did not seem overly concerned. "I believe sometimes it is just that way. Have you ever played with yourself? Put your fingers inside or used something like the dildo? It's all right if you did, for I would want you to lay back and show us how you pleased yourself."

I shook my head. "No. I've never touched myself like that. Only...only with you have I felt this way."

All three of the men smiled and I felt the fear, the chill of it, ebb away.

"You're not mad?" she breathed.

"Nay, lass. This is so much better, for now we can take ye as we wish."

"I thought that was what you had been doing," I countered. "You even shaved me."

"Aye, but if your maidenhead had been there and it tore, you'd be verra sore. Are ye sore, lass?"

I shook my head. I was...needy.

"Then it is going to be a long night, for our cocks are eager to fill you, to mark you, to make you ours." Simon and Cross traded places, and I remembered Simon said he would be first.

Cross angled me back on his arm to kiss me, his tongue plunging into my mouth directly and I tasted myself on his tongue; it was so carnal to learn the flavor of my own desire. His hand was on the back of my neck, holding me just as he wanted me and he overwhelmed me. His own need was obvious in his touch, his kiss, his very breath.

When he pulled back, his breathing was rough. "Lay back now and let us have our way with you."

I was so relieved they believed me that I did as he bid without question, although the kiss had certainly helped. I wanted to please them and clearly I became upset if I couldn't, or if I perceived some flaw in myself that would have them finding me deficient. But Cross' mouth was red and slick from our kiss and his eyes held secret promises I wanted to learn. The only way to do that was to lay back and let them teach me.

All three of them shifted to give me room, and Cross was kissing me once again, Rhys returned his attentions to my breasts

—he seemed to have a slight fixation with them—and Simon nudged my thighs apart with his hands and flicked his tongue over the place where Cross' thumb had been rubbing.

They were definite warriors, all of them, for they gave all their energies to a task and if they wanted to defeat their opponent, they could do so with sheer will alone. While I was not the enemy, they definitely laid siege and I could not uphold any of my defenses against them, not that I even wanted to. My head fell back and my eyes closed as the delicious pinch on my nipples set my body on fire. A hint of perspiration coated my skin as they again built me up to the brink of that sweet pleasure. They'd given it to me several times now and I recognized what it felt like just beforehand. I cried out and I could feel my belly tighten, my knees squeeze Simon's dark head for I did not wish him to move from that pleasure   spot.   I   wanted   him   to   stay right...there...and...lick...one...more...time. Yes!

I screamed my release, every muscle in my body tensing, my back arching off the bed, my inner walls clenching down on nothing...that thin dildo had just been a quick tease. They didn't stop their attentions, only Cross stopped kissing me but instead stroked a hand gently over my hair and crooned to me.

You are so beautiful. I love to see you come.

I felt a dip in the bed just before Simon's knees nudged my thighs wide as he settled into the cradle of my hips, his cock slipping over my slick woman's core. I was still coming, the luscious feelings making my heart pound, the blood roaring in my ears, as the large head stretched my opening as he slowly pushed his way in.

"Yes!" I cried, my inner walls now having something to clench onto.

"Christ, ye are so bloody tight."

I looked up at Simon, his eyes so dark as to be black. His hair fell over his forehead and his face was all hard lines, his neck tightly corded. He held himself up on his forearms, the hair on his chest tickling my breasts and tormenting my nipples. Rhys and Cross were watching, hands stroking their cocks.

Slowly, Simon slipped into me, one delicious inch at a time. While I'd just come, the new sensation of being stretched wide, being filled deeper and deeper had my arousal simmering. My body was soft and pliant and I brought my legs up to Simon's hips, giving him room to go even deeper. Finally, his hips bumped into my bottom and he was fully seated.

My eyes widened at the feel of him and he watched me carefully.

"Am I hurting ye?" he asked, his voice as dark and rumbly as a thunderstorm.

I shook my head and clenched down on him, testing my body.

"Nay, dinna do that unless ye want me to move."

I grinned and did it again. He groaned and gritted his teeth. "I want you to move."

His eyes flew open and he grinned, his blinding smile combined with the dark intent in his eyes had me eager.

"I *need* you to move, Simon."

And so he did, slowly at first, but when I arched up to meet him, tilted my hips into his thrusts, he didn't hold back.

I wrapped my legs around his waist and held onto his shoulders. "Yes!" I cried out, his cock rubbing over new places deep within me that had me back to the brink within seconds. He rubbed over my clit with each stroke and I just broke, coming again while Simon continued to move. It was so much better than ever before, the way his body could make me come, knowing that it was because we were joined, that his cock being so deep inside me. I screamed, for I could not hold it back. I felt my body soften and get even wetter, the sound of our joining loud. Simon's breathing was ragged and all at once he stiffened, embedded all the way and groaned. I felt his hot seed, the thick emission I'd stroked from him in the stable just that morning, flood my womb, coating me and marking me. There was no doubt I was his.

He kissed me gently, his breathing mixing with mine as he settled. While he was still inside of me, I could feel the wetness seeping out around him and when he pulled out, I whimpered.

"I'm speechless, lass," he said standing up before me. I was too replete to close my legs as I looked at his cock, slick and wet from our combined fluids, still hard. His face lost that tenseness and his smile was soft. He appeared very satisfied and I felt a surge of...something at knowing I was the one to make him that way.

Rhys moved off the bed to stand before me, his cock weeping clear fluid from the tip as his hand gripped the base. "I love this view. Our wife, sated from coming, our seed all over your pretty pussy. My turn, love."

He settled in between my thighs, his cock nudging my inner thigh. Up on his hand, he looked down at me. "Sore?"

I shook my head, anxious and ready for his turn. He took one leg and lifted my knee up to his hip, aligned his cock at my entrance and slid all the way in in one long, smooth stroke.

"Oh!" I gasped. This angle was different than how Simon had me. The feel of Rhys' cock was different and when he began to move, I recognized that he fucked differently as well. Simon had been gentle, perhaps because of his large size he had been afraid to hurt me, but when he let his baser needs take over, he became rougher, but even then he hadn't hurt me.

Rhys' motions were more deliberate, as if he knew just how to use his cock to bring me to pleasure as fast as possible. He was almost ruthless in his attentions, precise in his motions. "So hot and slippery wet. You feel incredible."

I smiled at him and he lowered his head to kiss me as his hips moved, filling me again and again.

"You'll come for me."

He said it as if I didn't have a choice. Perhaps I didn't, for he used his cock like a weapon and I was powerless against it. I could do nothing but give in, and so I did. As I tensed and tried to hold him within me, he came on a harsh stroke, a guttural sound escaping his lips that were sealed over mine.

When he pulled out of me, a gush of seed slipped from me and he stood before me, just as Simon had, proud of that fact.

"It's Cross' turn, lass. Ye dinna want him to feel neglected, do ye?" Simon sat on the edge of the bed, his back resting against the brass railed footboard. Only Cross looked tense between the three of them and I now knew why.

"Up," Cross said.

Slowly, as my muscles were as soft and loose as pulled taffy, I came up and onto my knees, the seed sliding down my thighs. Cross looked down at it and slid a finger through the wetness. "I'm going to add to this," he vowed.

Moving to the head of the bed, he sat with his back propped up against the pillows. "How are you at riding a horse?" he asked.

I frowned in confusion. "Quite well."

He grinned and held out his hand. "Good. Consider me your stud horse and take me for a ride."

I glanced down at Cross' cock, thick and erect and very ready to fuck.

"Straddle his legs," Rhys directed.

I took Cross' hand and crawled up the bed so that I had my knees on either side of his hips.

"Work yourself down onto my cock."

Placing a hand on his shoulder for balance, I met Cross' pale eyes as I shifted my hips so that the tip of his cock slid over me, then settled at my opening. With all of the other men's seed on me, it was not difficult to have him fill me. My eyes widened at the feel of him coming up and into me. This was so different than when I was on my back. I could look at Cross, see his expression as my body accepted him and opened for him. When he was fully embedded, I sat completely upon his thighs and we both groaned.

"Now, Olivia. Please. I've been patient, but no longer, for you feel too damn good. Ride me and ride me hard. I want to see your breasts move as you do, I want to see you come."

Carefully, I lifted back up as I bit my lip, wanting to do it right. I saw the heat flare in Cross' eyes. When I took him into me again, I bumped my clit on his body and I moaned, shifting my hips and almost grinding myself onto him. I wanted not only to be filled, but my clit to be worked. The combination had me moving; I had no choice for my body took over, my needs replaced my thoughts and so I moved blindly, mindlessly to what felt good.

I knew the other men were watching. I knew I was taking what I wanted from Cross. I knew they might think me wanton, my breasts bouncing as I moved so aggressively, but I didn't care. I'd been fucked twice already and knew they were passionate men and that they'd unleashed the passion within me. And so I used Cross' cock to my needs over and over until I was screaming, gripping his shoulders so hard he'd have indentations there surely.

My eyes flew open at the sheer intensity of the angle and the way it rubbed over new places.

Cross hissed. "She's milking my cock. I can't hold back. Take it, love, take it all," Cross growled.

He thrust his hips up and against me, filling me like a geyser, erupting up and into my womb, flooding me in his own wash of hot seed. I fell forward onto his chest, my sweaty breasts and belly slick against his. I tried to catch my breath as I listened to his heartbeat begin to slow. I could do nothing, nothing at all, for I was done in by pleasure. I didn't know whose hands were stroking my back and I didn't care, for I knew that while they were individuals, they claimed me as one. While it may be one man's hand on my back, they were all soothing me. It was my last thought as I fell into sleep.

12

$\mathcal{S}$IMON

"Good morning, lass."

Olivia stirred in my arms, her arse rubbing against my already hard cock. After she'd fallen asleep, I'd tucked her beneath the covers and settled in behind her, an arm over her waist, my hand cupping her breast perfectly. I should have had a difficult time sleeping as I was unused to sharing a bed, but I found having her tucked in safely with me was enough to put me into a sound sleep. I was accustomed to being awakened by nightmares, the sheets a tangle about my sweat soaked body as I awoke on a groan or sob, but my night was quiet, my mind at ease.

She stiffened briefly, and then, most likely realizing where she was and who was holding her, she relaxed. "Hello," she replied, her voice shy. "Where are the others?"

"We willna be together all of the time. They are asleep in their own beds."

"You will take turns with me?"

I shrugged, and then frowned at the idea. "You make it sound as if ye are a toy and we are a bunch of children."

She turned in my hold to look up at me, her pale eyes clear and alight with humor. "Yes, I believe that is an apt description."

I could not help but push her onto her back and prop myself above her. As we stirred, her sweet scent along with the tang of sex swirled around us. It was a heady mix, reminding me that she was soft and lush and feminine as well as the vixen we did all of the things to the night before.

"Dinna ye wish to get to know me?" I asked.

She nodded into the pillow. "You're the brawny one." She ran her small hand down over my chest and I sucked in my muscles of my belly as her hand worked lower, but didna touch my cock. She was nae forward yet in her wants, but she would be soon enough. "I also think you are the brooder, the one who worries the most."

She was insightful and that had me looking away, afraid she might see all the answers in my eyes. While Rhys had seen cruelty in the regiment, he hadna been there the day Evans slaughtered that family. I had and it affected me still. Even though our friend, Ian, was man pinned with the crime, the event followed more than just him halfway around the world.

"I take my responsibilities seriously, ye ken, and they now include ye. Are ye sore?" I lifted up off her enough to look down her naked body. Her breasts were coral tipped and just begging to be licked and sucked. The flesh between her thighs, now bare and smooth, surely ached to be stroked.

She cupped my chin and forced my head back up to meet her steady gaze. "You are changing the subject. You don't have to protect me from everything," she replied.

My heart hurt, actually ached at her simple statement. While I always had Rhys and Cross to watch out for me, this tiny slip of a woman was volunteering to be my protector as well.

"My little lioness," I whispered. "Dinna worry, lass, for tis just my dreams that haunt me. Enough about me, ye didna answer my question. Are ye sore?"

She continued to look at me for a few more moments, and then replied. "My body aches...down there, but I'm not sore."

"When I plow a field, me back hurts the next day." I brushed her dark hair back from her face. "When I plow yer field," she slapped my arm and I grinned, "ye are the one who is aching."

"Simon," she replied, eyes rolling.

"I bet ye are aching for my touch, for my cock."

She glanced away, but I turned her chin back. "Nay lass, now it is you who must answer the difficult question. Ye dinna need to be embarrassed. Yer body, when we are alone, it belongs to me."

Her pale eyes widened and she licked her lips. "I...I feel empty."

I couldn't help the groan that escaped and I shifted my hips so my cock rubbed up against her belly. "Do you want yer pussy filled?"

She bit her lip, glanced up at me through her dark lashes, then shyly nodded.

What my wife wanted, I gave.

———

CROSS

"I don't think three days is going to be enough," I said, washing the dinner dishes. It had been two days since we brought Olivia to the ranch and tomorrow we would have to share her with the others by joining everyone for lunch. "Surely Emma, Ann and Laurel are driving their men crazy with the waiting."

"Making Olivia come is more of a priority than satisfying the other ladies' eagerness to meet her. Each of them only has two men to share; Olivia has three. We *should* get an extra day," Rhys grumbled.

"It isna as if we have to give her up, just take her to lunch," Simon replied. "I'm glad a trunk was picked up in town, for now she has some of her things. The smile on her face when Andrew delivered it was verra pleasing. Now she'll be comfortable in clothes."

I groaned at the idea of her clothed again since she'd been mostly naked for the past two days.

"We eat lunch, then we can bring her home and fuck her," Simon added.

"You two have each had a night with her." I could hear the crankiness of my voice. Hell, it wasn't crankiness; it was unrequited lust. "I had to lay in my own bed knowing she was naked and warm...without me. What the hell did you do with her in the middle of the night?" I asked Rhys, whose smile spread wide.

"She went to the wash room and when she returned, I had her bend over the side of the bed and fucked her from behind. You could have joined us. You could have taught her how to suck your cock."

I could easily picture Olivia naked and leaning on the side of the bed, her ass up, her legs spread so her bare pussy was visible, then taking her. I also thought of her mouth opened wide around my cock. I groaned and turned back to the dishes, washing them with extra vigor.

"That wasn't what you heard, though," he added. I glanced over my shoulder at him and he was now sharing details just to taunt me, his grin a giveaway. "The sounds she made were when I worked the plug into her arse. It was her first one. It wasn't very big, but she's tight there. I kept it in as I fucked her, and then the rest of the night. It's going to be sweet when we get a cock in there. So bloody sweet and tight."

I couldn't handle the torment any longer. I put the dish down, wiped my hands on my pants and stormed down the hall.

"Be sure to use the next sized plug on her tonight," Rhys called to me as Simon laughed.

"We're taking her together from now on. I don't like to wait my turn," I called back.

I took the stairs two at a time to the washroom. Olivia was taking another bath—we were making her dirty quite frequently —and I entered the room with only a brief knock.

She didn't cover herself this time. That was what I noticed first. She'd lost a bit of her inhibitions, but the blush on her cheeks indicated she was clinging to her innocence. After what Rhys did to her last night and what I planned for tonight, she wouldn't be innocent for much longer.

"I heard you are taking Rhys' plugs in your ass."

She flushed even more furiously as she stood in the tub, water sluicing down her body. I held out my hand to help her out and grabbed the bath sheet as I did and began to dry her. "Well?" I asked.

"You seem angry."

I shook my head and knelt down to dry one leg, then the other. Her smooth, bare pussy was in perfect alignment with my face and my mouth watered to taste her. "Not angry. Eager. Eager for you. It's my turn to play."

"Don't I ever get to play with you?"

I paused, my hands on her legs and looked up her luscious body to meet her eyes. "Haven't you been playing all this time?"

"Yes, but you three tell me what to do."

I began to dry her again, my hands slow so I could savor the feel of her. "You mean you want to be in charge."

She thought for a moment. "Yes, perhaps I do."

I stood and dried her belly, then her breasts, where I lingered. I loved the lush shape of them, their weight, the way the plump nipples tightened at the slightest touch. "Your ass training is not up for negotiation."

"But—"

I silenced her with a finger over her lips.

"Don't you want the three of us to take you at the same time?"

I pulled my finger away and she replied, "Yes."

"Then we need to prepare your ass to take a cock. You know we're big. We don't want to hurt you. Remember, nothing but pleasure." With that resolved, I continued, "We will get the next size plug settled into that delectable ass of yours, and then you can be in charge. All night long."

"The plug needs to stay in that long?" she asked, quirking one dark brow.

"At least a few hours. I have needs though, love, so if you're in charge, it's your job to meet them."

13

OLIVIA

"How do you handle three men?" Emma asked, all dark hair and wide eyes.

She was married to Kane and Ian, who met us at their front door. From their accents, the men were English and Scot, just like Rhys and Simon and, from what I'd been told, had been in the same army regiment. Ann was equally interested to meet me, along with Laurel, and they'd pulled me into the kitchen away from the men. Ann was fair-haired and petite, while Laurel had fiery red hair and green eyes. They had me sit at the kitchen table and chop carrots as they moved about, cooking, stirring, checking if something was done baking.

I was not overly adept in the kitchen; I could make a simple meal for Uncle Allen and myself, but I couldn't handle a meal for fifteen, so I was content with the basic task they put before me. From what they told me, everyone at Bridgewater ate meals together—except when a group of them got married and didn't get out of bed for three days—and rotated the role as cook and dishwasher. While it seemed odd that they always ate at Kane, Ian and Emma's house, theirs was the largest and had, it seemed, been built with an overly large dining room for just this purpose. The only unmarried men left were Simon's brother and a man named MacDonald, both of whom had not arrived for lunch yet when I'd been dragged off. The ladies volunteered to cook today, clearly in order to get me alone and pepper me with questions.

"I don't know any other way," I replied. While I grew up imagining one husband, having three was the only way I knew.

"True, but men are fairly needy. Aren't you tired?" Ann asked, and then blushed. She had been married the longest to her husbands who were Robert and Andrew. They had an eight-month-old son who had been crawling on the floor under the supervision of his fathers, who'd introduced themselves as I walked by. "Surely you're tired if you are newly wed to those three."

They all giggled.

"Brody and Mason didn't let me out of bed for two days," Laurel said. She had wed in the winter, and from the story she told, was thankful to be alive since her men had rescued her from a blizzard.

"It seems," I started, then chopped through a large carrot with a loud thwap, "while they like to...to—"

I couldn't go on, for it was hard enough to get used to intimacy with the men, let alone talk about it with these women.

"You can share. We are very open at Bridgewater," Emma said. "My first day on the ranch Kane and Ian shaved my pussy and put a plug in my bottom with Laurel's husband right outside the door."

My mouth fell open. "Outside the—"

Laurel nodded and rolled her eyes. "He didn't see anything. If we need tending, our men make us their top priority."

95

I frowned. "I think my three are more private. While they like to share, they each also like to spend time alone with me," I admitted. "That's why it's been three days. While they...took me together," I blushed, but continued, "they also wanted time alone with me."

"See? They are needy," Ann commented.

"You are happy?" Emma asked. A baby's cry came from upstairs and she smiled. "Ellie's awake."

"Don't you have to get her?"

Emma shook her head and began to undo the bodice of her dress. "No. Kane and Ian dote on her terribly. One little whimper and they are checking on her. One of them will bring her down to me since she's hungry. Now, before they get here, are you happy?"

I thought about that. Rhys, Cross, and Simon had been nothing but kind to me. Attentive, thoughtful, aggressive, dominant, passionate.... The list was long, but none of them, except perhaps them sticking a plug that Rhys had made into my bottom, but otherwise...I *was* happy.

"So far, yes," I replied, for I thought that was a safe answer. There was a niggle of concern though, for the men were quite secretive. They knew much more about me than I did of them. That could be resolved over time, but not if they didn't share.

"I have a feeling they had difficult pasts," I surmised.

We heard heavy footsteps and silly talk at the same time.

"That would be Ian and Ellie," Emma said, smiling as she adjusted her dress and shift so her breast was exposed. "He's a big brawny man but melts as soon as he gets near his daughter."

In came Ian cradling a baby in his big arms. While Ellie was three months old, she appeared tiny being held by such a large man. He was crooning something to her in a different language, perhaps Gaelic. He kissed the baby's dark hair, much the same shade as her mother's, then handed her off. Emma settled her against her breast. Ian watched his wife and baby for a moment, leaned in and kissed the top of Emma's head almost reverently, then left.

Watching Emma with one of her doting husbands made me feel wistful. While Uncle Allen had doted on me and loved me, he'd had a secret family on the side, one he hadn't wished to include me in. Yes, I'd been involved with the Tannenbaums from the beginning, even being friends with their son, Tyler, who had moved to Billings the year before.

Tyler was two years old than I was, and we'd grown up together. His parents doted on him, but the Tannenbaums weren't his only parents. He had Uncle Allen, too. Was he Tyler's father, and I had never known it? They'd kept me on the periphery all this time. Surely Tyler knew the arrangement of his parents—two fathers and a mother, perhaps he'd even known we were actually cousins—while I hadn't known a thing. My parents had died in a stage accident, leaving me behind on their way to Bozeman.

Finding out about Uncle Allen's secret life had left me feeling somehow betrayed, as if I'd been an outsider all along.

I felt like an outsider now as I watched Emma, Ian and their baby. The bond was there between them, and with Kane as well. The other women had a place on the ranch, each of them a loving life with their men. But me? I was lost. I felt...extraneous and out of sorts. I didn't really know anything about Rhys, Cross or Simon and that only added to my discomfort.

Once Emma had the baby settled down to nurse, they glanced at each other, then at me. The meal was forgotten, at least for the moment. "You asked after their pasts. I think they've all had hardships, Ian especially." Emma looked both wistful and angry, probably because she wanted to protect her man from the burdens of his past, but couldn't. "I've heard some of what happened to them—Simon and Rhys—in Mohamir, for Ian is the one wanted for the crimes he didn't commit," Emma told me, her voice bitter. "But none of the men have shared details of what the crimes actually are, other than that their commander, Evans, killed innocent people."

"Simon woke up from a nightmare the other night, calling out the word *alea*, but I don't know what it means, or if it is something in that country's language or a name. When I asked if he was all right, he said 'dinna worry yerself' and held me as he fell back asleep." I shrugged. "He just seems to carry the past with him more heavily than most. Cross, too. He wasn't even with them in Mohamir. He's hinted at a terrible childhood, but again, he won't tell me more."

They all held secrets, it seemed. *Everyone* held secrets from *me*.

Laurel looked understanding. "Your men are more reserved, as we don't know much either. They'll tell you in time, if they choose. Just be there for him, tend to them as much as they tend to you. They might be big and formidable, especially Simon, but they have their weaknesses, they just don't show them often."

"Don't forget the biscuits," Emma reminded Laurel, who went to the oven to check on them.

"Their biggest weakness is now Olivia," Ann said, moving out of the way for Laurel as she stirred a pot on the stove. "They've taken on your enemy as their own."

When we arrived for lunch, Rhys told everyone about how we met, the threat to my life by Mr. Peters and now I felt guilty, for in truth, besides protecting me through marriage, my men would also have to defend against anything he might do. They'd assumed my burdens, even though they seemed to carry plenty of their own. Had they done this because they felt guilt at buying the horse from the man who may have burned down my house?

"I'm glad it doesn't bother you that the stud horse they

purchased came from him," Laurel said, passing by me with a handful of cloth napkins to place on a tray.

I paused in the middle of a cut, knife in the air. While I hadn't forgotten that the men bought the horse from Mr. Peters, I'd put it to the back of my mind. It raised questions I hadn't considered before - questions that only now came about as I was married and entrenched in Bridgewater.

I stood and offered a small smile, wiping my hands together. "Will you excuse me for a moment?"

The ladies looked at me with surprise since I'd abruptly stood and wanted to leave in the middle of a conversation, but nodded. I left the kitchen and followed the men's voices to the room off the front entry. Comfortable chairs faced a cold fireplace. With eleven men in the room, they sat in the chairs but also leaned against the wall, relaxed and in easy conversation. When they saw me, they stood. While they all looked at me, the only men whose gazes held heat and possession were my three.

Rhys came over to me first, followed by Cross and Simon. "Is everything all right?" Their gazes raked over me as if confirming nothing had happened to me in the short duration I was out of their sight.

"Why did you keep Mr. Peter's horse?" I asked.

Simon's brow quirked at the question. "Is there something wrong with the animal?" he asked.

I shook my head. "He seems a fine horse, but if you dislike the man who sold him to you so much, why do business with him?"

"We didna know his actions toward ye before the deal was done," Simon said. "Remember, I hadna met you at the dance as these blokes had, for I was with Peters at the saloon." He didn't seem happy about it either.

I remembered the first time I saw Simon—outside in front of my house in just my robe—and how he'd looked at me with worry and something else. I didn't know it then, but the look was most definitely lust.

"Yet you gave your money to a man I dislike, whom my uncle dislikes, and from what I understand, you don't like him either."

Rhys leaned against the back of a chair so we were of similar height. "We wanted the horse, not him. Our relationship with the bloody man is done."

"Why do business with such a...bloody man?" I put my hands on my hips. "You know how I feel about him."

"Do you want us to return the horse, is that what you're asking?" Cross asked. "Are you making us choose between you and the horse?"

Was I? I felt irrationally angry all of a sudden, as if they were content giving money to a man who was so...dishonorable.

"I just didn't consider it before now, as you are all so mind-consuming." Wicked grins spread across all three men's faces. "It just seems as if you are condoning his behavior."

Rhys narrowed his eyes in thought.

"And we are condoning your behavior right now," Rhys countered. "What's the matter, love? You seem as if you're itching for an argument. You've known ever since the dance we bought the stud horse from him and have not mentioned a concern before now. If you need attention, love, all you had to do was ask."

"I am not—"

Rhys held up his hand.

"We are a large group and I would think daunting for you," Cross said. He looked to Simon, who nodded.

"We were going to take ye home and fuck ye good and hard, but it seems ye canna wait." Simon reached for her hand. "Come, we will fuck ye now."

14

$\mathcal{O}$LIVIA

Simon tugged me across the room, the other two following. "What? Wait!" I dug my heels in but there was no way I could compete with Simon in strength. "We can't...I mean, the men, they're all staring!"

Heat flooded my cheeks at the thought. Simon pulled me out of the room, down the hall and into what appeared to be an office. I could barely hear the men's voices from the other room and we were on the opposite side of the house from the kitchen. Rhys closed the door behind him, and I was surrounded by my men with nowhere to go. The room seemed so small with them looming.

"I don't need to be fucked now, truly. Let's go back out there before they start thinking that's what we are doing in here."

"Nay, lass, ye're getting your fucking now."

"But—"

"We may be many here at Bridgewater, but the four of us are a family," Cross said. "You are the center of our world even if we are not in the room with you."

While I believed *he* believed in what he said, I doubted him. I wasn't the center of Uncle Allen's world. I thought I had been, but I wasn't.

"We are newly wed and if we must continue to prove this to you until you believe it, then we will," Rhys said, forcing me to walk backward until I bumped into the large desk. "Turn around, love."

Simon stood next to Rhys, but Cross went around to the other side of the desk and moved the chair out of the way. When I didn't respond as he bid, Rhys put his hands on my waist and spun me about. A large hand on my back had me bending forward over the wooden surface of the desk.

Cross began undoing the front placket of his dark pants and his cock sprung free—his hard, thick cock, clear fluid seeping from the tip. The broad head was plush and I licked my lips with the idea of tasting it.

"I told him how you learned to suck cock, love, and how you took me so deep into your mouth I couldn't help but come on your tongue. Show Cross how good you are."

I felt hands on my legs and cool air on my skin as my dress was lifted.

"You sucked Rhys' cock?" Cross asked, moving forward so the tip of his cock nudged against my lips. "Part those lips and take me into your mouth. I've been dying to be inside there."

"The others...they'll know," I said, glancing up, way up at Cross.

"Don't worry, my cock will stifle all of your cries of pleasure when Rhys and Simon fuck you."

Those words had my pussy becoming wet. Wetter, actually, for I was always wet. With Cross' insistent nudging of his cock, I opened and took him into my mouth. The fluid at the tip tasted salty and clean and made my mouth water. I ran my tongue over the large vein that ran along the bottom, and then sucked on him, just as Rhys had taught me.

"Jesus, Olivia, you're going to make me come like a randy teenager."

I basked in the warmth of his words, as well as the way his hand stroked over my hair, knowing I was pleasing him. I heard as much as felt my drawers rip before sliding down my legs.

"No more drawers, lass," Simon said. "They are just in the way."

Hands stroked over my bottom and I felt the slight weight of my dress bunched at my waist just before hands slid over my pussy, separating my folds before he plunged his cock deep into me. My hips arched up at the abrupt, yet decidedly wonderful action, my moan of pleasure and surprise muffled, just as Cross had said, by his cock that was deep in my mouth.

"You wanted our attention, love, so we are going to give it to you. Simon's first."

The finger pulled free with a loud wet sound and I felt the blunt tip of a cock at my opening, but it didn't linger there or tease me, only slid in with one decisive stroke. I moaned at the feeling, so full, so deep, so perfectly fitting.

"If I hadn't told you, love, that Simon would fuck you first, you wouldn't have known. All of our cocks belong cramming you full. You'll take any one of us at any time because you are our wife," Rhys dictated. "We will give you whatever you need, whatever you desire, whenever you need it."

Smack.

My eyes widened and I cried out around Cross' cock. Simon spanked me! While I tried to pull my mouth free, Cross held me in place and began to slowly move his cock in and out of my mouth instead of me sucking on him as he liked.

"We're here, lass, and nae going anywhere."

Smack.

"If ye need me to spank your arse for you to recognize that, then that's what I'll do."

Smack.

"Did it ever occur to ye, lass, that we didn't give the horse back to Peters—" *Smack* "—because he would then know ye are here with us? Keeping a horse belonging to that bastard is like a sliver under a nail, but we will see ye safe first."

Smack.

I didn't have more than a moment to think about his words, for his hips thrust faster and harder and then I couldn't think at all. My hands flattened against the cool wood, but there was nothing to grab on to, to keep me grounded, as I could no longer fight anything they did. I didn't want to.

"I'm going to come, Olivia, and you're going to swallow my seed. All of it. You're going to taste me on your tongue, to know that I gave you what you needed."

He thrust into me gently one more time, and I felt him swell just before a hot jet of seed coated my tongue and slid down my throat. Again and again his cock pulsed in my mouth as his fingers clenched my scalp.

Simon didn't relent on his driven thrusts, the sound of his hips smacking against my bottom loud in the room.

Cross slowly pulled his cock from my mouth; it was slick and glistening, only diminishing in size slightly before he tucked it back in his pants.

A hard thrust pushed my hips into the desk as Simon let out a groan. His seed was warm and copious enough for me to feel it deep inside. When he was spent and pulled free, his essence slipped down over my clit, onto my thighs and most likely the desk below.

I looked over my shoulder and saw Rhys holding his rigid cock and moving into position between my spread legs. He used his hand to scoop up the seed that had escaped, and rubbed it into my swollen, sensitive flesh. They were right; I was so much more aroused by the smooth, shaved skin.

He took his dripping fingers and moved them to my back entrance, began playing with me there, coating me again and again with Simon's seed. I was so aroused, so needy from Simon's cock and expert fucking that I felt empty and almost forlorn without something filling my pussy. But when Rhys carefully worked a finger into my back entrance and the nerves there came to life, instant heat washed over me, and my brow and temples became damp with perspiration. I couldn't help the groan that escaped, for the jangly, dark feelings that came from his ass play felt so good. I couldn't fight him, couldn't fight the feelings he wrung from my body.

"Here," Rhys said. I saw Cross take something from him over my back and hold it in front of my face so I could see it. It was another one of his handcrafted plugs. He'd used them on me before to stretch me open in preparation for all of them to take me at once, but this one was different. While the other two had been fairly thin and meant for them to play with me—to fuck me there with them without much discomfort yet with plenty of sensation —this plug was quite wide in the middle, the flared head just a narrow tip then broadened quite a bit, then tapered in again, a flat flange at the base for Cross' fingers.

I winced when Rhys slipped a second finger in me along with the first. "I was going to save this for later, but I think now is a better time."

Cross handed it back and I turned my head to follow it. Rhys took it and held it up for me to see one last time, for I knew its destination.

"You're going to love this," he promised. I wasn't as certain, especially when he slipped his fingers free. I thought he was going to push it right into my bottom, but he didn't. I heard a jar open and I knew it was the special ointment to coat the plugs and dildos so they could slide easily—easier—into me.

"You aren't the only one who has their arse filled, lass," Simon said. "Good thing Ian and Kane have jars of the slick lubricant all over the house for Emma."

I only thought for a moment about Emma being placed in the same position as I and having her bottom filled, perhaps not with a plug but her men's cocks. They'd been married long enough for her to be able to be fucked there. Perhaps I'd ask her about it when—

"Oh!" I cried, the cold, blunt and very slippery plug nudged against my back entrance.

Rhys expertly twisted and pushed and worked it into me, wider and wider and wider until I didn't think I could take anymore. "Rhys, please," I groaned.

Just after I uttered the words, the plug narrowed again and my muscles clenched tightly around the narrow section. The wide, hard portion filled me so differently than ever before. It was wide like a cock but not deep, and stretched my opening as the other plugs had. Outside of me, I could feel the cool flat wood parting my cheeks slightly but holding the plug securely within. Rhys tugged on the base and I groaned once again. With my bottom so full, my pussy felt empty.

Perhaps Rhys was a mind reader, for he said, "Is your pussy lonely, love? Let's get you all filled up."

Within seconds I felt his cock at the entrance to my pussy and sliding in, much slower than Simon, but there hadn't been a large plug in my bottom at the same time. Simon moved to stand beside

Cross and they both squatted down so their faces were right before mine.

When Rhys' cock bottomed out, the flared head nudging my womb, my eyes widened. I'd never felt so full. I moaned. They grinned.

"Like having something in your arse and pussy? Soon enough we'll have one of our cocks in your pussy, another in your arse and another in this perfect mouth," Simon leaned forward and kissed me, my breath coming out in quick pants as Rhys began to fuck me at a vigorous pace.

"The plug is making her so tight," Rhys said through gritted teeth. "I'm not going to last."

"Are you ready to come, Olivia?" Cross asked. I nodded, for the way Rhys' hips bumped into the base of the plug every time he filled me—how snug he was when he did so—had him rubbing and bumping and nudging places inside me that were new, that were so hot, so intense I couldn't hold back.

"You may come." Cross' voice was soothing, yet commanding. "Show us your pleasure. Squeeze Rhys' cock when you do."

Perhaps it was Cross' words or the erotic feel of being fucked and filled so completely, but I came with a scream, so lost in the flood of heat and pleasure that coursed through me that I forgot all about where I was and who might hear. I tossed my head back, my eyes fell closed and my muscles tensed, as if I held still the feelings would never end. Rhys gripped my hips in his firm hold and held me in place as he thrust deep one last time, a growl escaping his throat as he filled me to overflowing. He leaned forward, slapping a hand on the table beside mine and kissed my sweaty neck, nuzzled against my ear before slowly pulling out.

I slumped onto the desk, my heated cheek savoring the cool wood. I could fall asleep just as I was, for I felt boneless and relaxed and blissfully sated. Cross and Simon stood to their full heights and came around behind me. I should be concerned at how I appeared, my pussy dripping with their seed, no doubt swollen and red, for it felt hot and well used. The plug was still tightly lodged within my bottom. I must have been quite a sight, but I didn't care. They were right; I had wanted their attentions, needed to have validation that I was wanted. How had they known even when I hadn't?

I pushed up onto my elbows, and then felt firm hands about my waist helping me up, and then holding me firmly as I settled. Simon looked down at me and grinned, kissing my forehead tenderly. "Let's eat, lass. I'm hungry as a bear."

Then I remembered my scream. "I...I can't go back out there, they'll know," I said.

Simon picked up my drawers from the floor and shoved them into his pants pocket, a hint of the white fabric peeking out, and winked at me. It seemed I wasn't to have them back.

"They do know, love, and trust me, they won't say a thing. All of them, at one time or another, except McPherson—Simon's brother, I mean, and MacDonald—have tended to their wives at one time or another near the others. You come first," Rhys replied.

"You're not embarrassed?"

Cross tilted my chin up. "Embarrassed for pleasing our woman so well that she screamed in pleasure? Definitely not. Quite the opposite, in fact."

Male preening did not help at all. "Can I clean up beforehand at least? Please take the plug out, Rhys, and let me have a cloth."

All three men shook their heads.

"No," Rhys said.

"Nay, lass," added Simon.

"You wanted our attention and you had it," Cross replied. "With the plug in your ass, their seed dripping from your pussy and the taste of mine on your tongue, will ensure you remember that we are always with you."

"Always," Rhys added, opening the door for me.

As we went out to join the others, walking carefully with the plug still settled deep. I wasn't soon going to forget.

15

$\mathcal{O}$LIVIA

Over the next few days, the men were extra attentive, ensuring that one of them was with me at all times. I had not recognized my need for their presence, or that I was worried that they, too, might leave me, but they had. While I could not blame my parents for their untimely deaths, I did blame them for leaving me. As for Uncle Allen, I couldn't deny him the woman he loved or the family he'd made. I couldn't be selfish. But what of Simon, Rhys and Cross? Would they want to leave me as well? Did I crave them in a way that had me taking their attention however I could get it, even if it were to bicker?

I wanted to be the center of their focus because *they* wanted to give it to me, not because I was needy, and that was the crux. It was hard to be confident in our slowly forming bond when I was fretting over something that was completely out of my control. And so when the men were all needed to help repair a large section of fence that had washed out in a mudslide overnight, they were concerned about leaving me alone. They even suggested I go and visit the other women, but truthfully, it had been hard to face them after the group lunch. They all might be comfortable with fucking or being tended to with the others nearby, but I was not. It would take time, and my men seemed to understand that and didn't push me.

When they left for the stable to meet the others, I promised I would walk to Laurel's if I got lonely, for her house was the closest. Once they left, I was content to just read, the windows and doors thrown open to the warm summer day. It also left me open to unwanted visitors.

The footsteps I heard in the hallway I thought could be Simon's, perhaps returning to take me one more time. It was his way to come to me, heat and lust in his eyes, because he couldn't wait another moment to have me. It was hot and my heart pounded and my pussy wept just knowing I made him so eager. Frantic, even.

So when I heard his footsteps this time, I started to undo the buttons of my dress in anticipation, for I knew how much he liked to suck and nip on my nipples as he fucked me. But the man that came into the den was not Simon, nor Rhys or Cross. It was Mr. Peters. I tugged the front of my dress together with one hand as I stood and backed away. The look on his face was almost gleeful, which scared me greatly.

"What...what do you want?" I asked.

"I'm not going to hurt you. I just want to talk."

Talk? Why would he come all the way to Bridgewater to talk? The man was lying and definitely insane.

"How did you find me?" I eyed him warily and very cautiously.

He studied me, tilting his head to the side as to look at me better. His scrutiny was hard to stand, but I did not flinch, did not fill the silence as I waited for his answer.

Finally, he spoke. "They haven't told you, have they?"

"They?" I asked, frowning.

"You married Simon, but I know the other two are fucking you as well. It was all part of my plan."

I swallowed down the fear at seeing him as my fingers fumbled with the buttons on my dress. I didn't want to be exposed in any way with him.

"Plan?" I couldn't manage more than one word questions and I disliked that fact. I should have the upper hand, I should show him the door, but I couldn't. I was too afraid. There was something about his voice, the look in his eye, his bearing, everything, that had me nervous and wary.

"Why do you think you're here? Your *men* belong to me."

I frowned even more deeply. "I don't understand."

"You rebuffed me, so I put men who belong to me in your path. You don't think Simon McPherson would be interested in the likes of you if not for a little incentive?"

The disdain in his voice had me flinching and the way his eyes roved over my body in disgust had me questioning Simon's touch, Rhys' words and Cross' wry humor.

He started laughing. "I can see that you did. I wanted your money, sweetheart, not you. If you weren't going to have me—and that crazy uncle of yours wouldn't let me get near you—then I'd get one of my men to have you instead. It was quite simple really. Simon gets a wife who will submit to his sick ways and fuck three men at once, along with a small payment for his efforts. By the look of you and the way you were stripping down just now, they have you well trained."

I wrinkled my nose in disgust. Had Simon only wanted me for some money and to have a woman to bed with his two closest friends? That couldn't be possible. It was obvious that Bridgewater was a successful ranch and wouldn't have married me for a little bit of money. It was possible he wanted a woman to share with Cross and Rhys, but all three of the men surely had never lacked in female attention and didn't need to marry to do that.

"Simon never even met me until right before we wed," I countered, trying to find issue with his account. "How would he have even met me in Helena?"

Mr. Peters looked down at his fingers as if bored. "He didn't have to. He used his friends to lure you in at the dance. I believe there are two men with whom you are shared?"

How did he know all of this? I remembered the feeling when I first laid eyes on Cross, then later, Rhys. Uncle Allen had used the word lightning, my heart lurching, my skin tingling, the feeling that everyone else in the room disappeared. They'd both been so confident in their attentions, so dominant and... so manly that I'd been almost distracted. The lightning had struck and my brain had lost clarity.

When I didn't respond, he continued. "Simon and I finalized the arrangement at the saloon while you were wooed at the dance. I just stopped in briefly to ensure the men were doing their job, but I had no need. It seems you were lured in quite easily."

A greasy feeling settled in my stomach as I remembered seeing him as I danced with Cross. "Simon works for you?"

The idea seemed preposterous, but here Mr. Peters was, in Simon's house and the story seemed...plausible. Doubtful, but plausible. He wanted something from me more than just talk and I had an idea what it was. I'd spurned his advances before, I doubted he'd let me do so now. I had to keep him talking.

"The horse was just a facade for the real business. *You.*" He chuckled. "Do you really think he needs another *horse*? A stud horse? *Simon's* the stud horse and you're the mare." He grinned at his crude words.

I skirted around him and toward the door. I had to get away. "Then why are you here? If you have what you want, my money, then why even come to Bridgewater?"

He was quicker than I expected. His rotund physique hid a quick step and he grabbed my arm in a talon-like grip. "To ensure you knew the truth. I don't allow anyone to say no to me. You did and your uncle protected you, so I have to punish you. Now you will live with the truth—that you're married to a man who only wanted your money, your body. The other two sick bastards? Simon McPherson thinks so little of you that he'll even share you like a common whore."

"How did you find me?" I'd thought I'd been hidden so well.

"I knew all along, of course. I just wanted to wait a few days to ensure the men had well and truly claimed you—which I can see they have." He glanced down at my bodice and my cheeks heated. "Also to let you know what your man is really like and you can live with the knowledge that I orchestrated it all."

His answer had me connecting pieces of the past week together as if it were a puzzle, one piece interlocking into another. His story actually fit, but I didn't believe it. I had to get away from the man but as I struggled, he backhanded me across the face, white spots dancing in my vision and the sharp sting of his strike made me wince.

"I'm also here to take what you refused to give before. If you already fuck three men, you should not object to one more."

I shook my head and fought him, clawing my hand down his face, my nails digging into his jowls. His hold loosened and I remembered Uncle Allen's advice regarding unwanted advances. I brought my knee up with all my might between his legs, hoping his cock would now be useless. He bent at the waist and a high-pitched sound came from his throat, his hand releasing me. I didn't linger, but fled down the hall and out the front door. I ran blindly toward the stable. I had to get away, away from Mr. Peters at all costs. I could go run home to Uncle Allen, but I had no home; it had been burned and Uncle Allen had his own family. My hair came unbound and my breath came out in deep pants. A stitch pained my side but I kept going. My men. I needed my men.

———

SIMON

While we fucked Olivia frequently and with thorough attention, we'd spent more time out of bed than in three days after our return to Bridgewater. We learned she was an accomplished rider and could herd cattle like a ranch hand with years in the saddle. She was well educated and could speak of books in the evening with Rhys, which fascinated me. I wasna book smart, but could appreciate a lively debate. As Cross showed her how to cook eggs without burning them, they laughed. and I reveled in the way her eyes brightened. I watched quietly, biding my time, for I was always ready to rip the buttons from her dress or toss up her skirts to test her readiness for my cock. She took to our rule of no drawers and it was verra pleasant reaching beneath her dress to find her bare, slick and ready.

Olivia and I didna talk much. We mostly fucked, for this was the connection we shared. If we came upon each other in a hallway, we didna speak, but grabbed each other with frantic, hands and kissed carnally, almost roughly, until I could lift and carry her to a place where I could fuck her. She'd even help, lifting her skirts for me or unbuttoning her bodice to offer her plush breasts. It was elemental and raw and when we were joined, we didna need any words. We were frantic for each other, almost desperate in our need to be close.

It wasna a deep connection like she had with Rhys or comfortable as what she had with Cross. We were more heat and fire, not needing to talk when all we wished to do was get naked— or as naked as we needed to be —for us to fuck. On occasion, Rhys or Simon would hear our rough coupling and join us, but it was I who got her hot, who was able to stoke the lust in those pale, expressive eyes.

After a day of moving rock and digging fence posts, we were all dirty, sweaty and hungry. All I wanted to do was bathe off all the mud and then sink into my wife.

Just this morning, she was verra fetching in her pale blue dress, a color that matched her eyes perfectly. I didna comment on it as Rhys had, but I had shown her how much I liked it by pressing her up against the kitchen door, dropping to my knees before her, lifting her skirts up high enough so I could lick and taste her bare pussy, working her with my fingers until she came, dripping all over my mouth and chin. Rhys and Cross had made breakfast and watched, and all of us agreed that upon our return from the repairs, we wanted her breasts out and on offer.

I didna feel right leaving her behind and unprotected, although I kent she was safe on the ranch; the other women remained at home as well by their men without concern. It wasna that they were less vigilant, for all of the men at Bridgewater put the women and children above all else, but I knew first hand what could happen if I relaxed in my duties to protect her.

While in Mohamir, we'd been tasked to watch over a Mohamiran diplomat and his family. I'd been assigned Alea, the sixteen-year-old daughter to guard. I was many years her senior and felt a keen need to protect her. There was no connection as I had with Olivia, not only because she was too young and our cultural differences too vast, but more because her father trusted me with her life.

We were no longer under the command of the fucking bastard, Evers, who'd singlehandedly murdered Alea and her family. I would not let Olivia down as I had Alea, as we all had her family. It was this incident, this dead family's faces that haunted me still. I was older, wiser and no longer in Mohamir. This was my job in this marriage, to ensure Olivia's safety, for she was a part of me. *She was mine.*

As we rode back to the ranch, one of the hands met us, his horse winded from the pace the man set.

He tilted his hat back. "Ann saw a man at your house. She said it could be Olivia's uncle, but she couldn't be sure."

I shook my head. "Nay. He wouldna come here and risk the bastard Peters following him."

We glanced at each other and spurred our horses toward the house. After a swift search, she wasna there. My gut clenched and I knew instantly something was wrong.

Rhys' eyes narrowed and his shoulders went back. His entire bearing changed. "The stables?" he asked.

'Twas possible, so I gave a curt nod and we both mounted and spurred our animals in that direction. When we rode up, dust kicking up around us, I called out to Kane, who was outside. "Is Olivia here?"

He shook his head. "Ian just came from our house. She's not there."

"Bloody hell," I muttered, glancing out and along the horizon. I tried not to clench my teeth, but I had the overwhelming feeling of helplessness. Where the bloody hell was she?

"Is there a horse missing?"

Kane turned on his heel and went to look.

"Christ," Cross muttered.

I looked up at the sky. About two more hours of daylight left. We had to find her, and soon.

Kane ran out, his feet sliding on the dusty ground. "The new stud horse is missing."

"We'll find her," I vowed, my fists clenching. "We just need to ken which way she went."

16

CROSS

If anyone could track Olivia, it was Simon. Not only did he have vast skill at the task, but he had motivation as well. He struggled to communicate, offering more scowls and brash action than tenderness; he was never known for kindness, but he was different with Olivia. He didn't open up to her more than anyone else, but he watched her in a way I hadn't seen before. Reverence, tenacity and a gentleness he may not have known he had. The two of them fucked with wild abandon, their connection deeper than anything I ever had with Olivia. We talked and joked and found a common friendship between us along with being lovers, but it was different with Simon. Because of that, I worried. I knew how he blamed himself in part for the murders in Mohamir; he hadn't known about the intended crime nor took part in it in any way, but he took his role as defender and protector seriously and he'd let his young charge down. She'd died under his supervision, even if it had been during a time when he was not on duty.

It had been over ten years ago and he still had nightmares; I often saw him at the breakfast table with dark circles and misery etched on his face. With Olivia, he took his concern for her safety to an extreme, even going to the greatest length of marrying her to protect her without having known her for more than a few minutes beforehand. He'd do anything for her, and I had to only hope she had come to no harm, for this would be something from which Simon would not recover.

"I'll go back to the house to see if she left a note or some other clue as to her whereabouts." Rhys grabbed the reins of one of the horses, mounted and turned toward the house.

Simon was tense and most likely ready to beat the face in of the mystery man, for he must know as readily as I, he was the basis for Olivia's disappearance.

"I'll confirm she's not at any of the houses. If I find her, I'll fire two shots," Kane said, mounting his horse, which most likely wanted a rubdown and some hay.

That left me alone with Simon.

"Let's start at the stall."

Simon strode off with single mindedness, his steps long. He stopped about ten feet from the door, and assessed the empty stall for a moment before entering. The hay was fresh on the ground, which meant the animal hadn't been in the stall the entire day. Turning on his heel, he went to the back sliding doors and pushed it open, letting the sun stream into the dim interior.

He glanced down at the dirt directly outside, the squatted down. "See this." He pointed to tracks in the dirt. "The horse was led this way."

I came down beside him, met his dark gaze. "You can tell just by looking at the horseshoes?"

He gave a simple nod. "Peters' horse only had them on the front. We put them on all four feet of ours, just havena done them yet for the stud horse. See, these here have no horseshoes."

Standing abruptly, he followed the tracks to the back pasture. "They continue out the gate." This direction wasn't the corral or even the near pasture but the western graze land for the cattle.

"We haven't had that horse this way before, have we?" I asked.

Simon shook his head. "We've kept him separate for now, so he hadna been out this way."

"This means—"

"Olivia came this way."

———

OLIVIA

The men should have returned to the ranch by now, but I was woefully lost. I'd fled, afraid Mr. Peters would follow, so I'd quickly put only a bridle on the new horse and rode it off in the direction I thought the men would be working. I'd been wrong in my direction. Very wrong, for the sun had just set and I had yet to find them.

I fought tears that I'd held at bay but when I knew I would not find my men before darkness fell, they slipped down my sweaty cheeks unbidden. Mr. Peters' appearance had scared me, for I'd been alone and he'd surprised me. I'd remembered the painful feel of his grip upon my wrist, the dark and sinister look in his eyes when I'd spurned him in Helena. The throbbing in my cheek prompted me continually to his danger. All I wanted was to find my men and accept the shelter they continually offered.

While Simon was the least communicative of the three, he was the most demonstrative. I felt a bond with Rhys and Cross as well, for they were able to share and show their connection through debates or humor, but with Simon, who was so staid and reserved, what we shared was...elemental. It couldn't be faked, it couldn't be bought as Mr. Peters had said; it couldn't be anything but real. So when Mr. Peters insinuated the worst, all I wanted to do was to get to my men, to have them hold me, reassure me. *Love me.* My hastiness was costly though. I didn't know where I was and none of the men did either. How could they find me if I didn't even know my own whereabouts?

Once I realized I had misjudged their location, I assumed it would be easy to find my way back, but I must have followed the wrong creek downstream and then became turned around. My dress had been fine for daytime, but the air was quickly cooling and the wind was picking up, whipping my hair into my face. Clouds had moved in, thick and heavy with the promise of rain, just as we'd seen the previous night. I had to find some kind of shelter. Unfortunately, the open prairie was not a safe place in bad weather and the few cottonwood trees that dotted the creek were a definite danger. Based on the severity of the mudslide the previous night, I knew that being near the water was not a choice so I spurred the horse up and away from the creek bed in case it swelled.

Large boulders dotted the landscape and I stopped and dismounted beside one of the larger ones. My first thought when I saw it was that it was the perfect height for my men to bend me over and fuck. While it couldn't shield me from rain, if I sat curled up on one side of it, the wind would be blocked. I shifted to sit sideways so I could lean against it, bent my legs up, wrapped my dress over my legs and put my head on my knees, holding onto the horse's lead with one hand.

I began to think of Rhys, Simon and Cross, their varied smiles, their varied kisses, their varied techniques with their cocks. I thought of their hands on my body, how they felt and the way I was beginning to recognize the differences between them, how they warmed my skin.

At first I thought I heard thunder, but it was actually the heavy beat of horse hooves that shook the ground. "Olivia!"

I didn't believe my ears, but when I heard my name a second time, I lifted my head. A group of men on horseback approached and I stood quickly. Elation flooded me, making me almost weak with relief. When Simon dismounted with the animal still moving, heading directly for me, I started to cry once again. I could tell by the fierce gaze, his clenched jaw and quick step that I'd been right in my thoughts and Mr. Peters was dead wrong.

He pulled me into him, his big hand cupping the back of my head against his chest. "Are ye hurt?" he asked, his voice rough.

The other men circled around me, their bodies blocking the wind. I glanced up at Rhys and Cross and I could easily read their relieved expressions.

Simon kissed the top of my head before pushing me back enough so that he could lean down and look me in the eye, and when he saw the tears on my cheeks, wiped them away with his thumbs. When he glanced at my cheek, his face hardened, the dark eyes of a warrior appeared. "Who hurt you?" A bruise must have formed on my cheek.

I tensed at the question. "Mr. Peters."

Simon's fingers tightened on my arms as he glanced at Rhys and Cross, then focused on me. "Did he hurt ye anywhere else? Did he—?"

I shook my head fiercely. "No. I got away."

The relief was visible, then his gaze roamed over my face with the tender look I'd been thinking of when I was lost. His dark gaze searching mine, as if he could see all the way to my soul. "He said disparaging things about you, but...but I didn't believe him and then I wanted to be with you."

He cupped my face and kissed me, pent up emotion and longing forged in that kiss. He eventually releasing me so Cross could pull me into his hold. By now, I was breathing hard, as if Simon had taken my breath away.

"What did he say?" Cross asked as he kissed the top of my head. His scent mixed with sweat and horses had me closing my eyes briefly to savor it.

"He said all three of you worked for him and that you made an arrangement so that Simon would marry me and give him my inheritance and you'd get a portion of it, along with me as a bonus."

Cross stilled his hand that was stroking up and down my back. "What else did he say?" His voice seemed to have dropped an octave.

"That you and Rhys were wooing me at the dance while Simon finalized their arrangements in the saloon," I added.

Rhys turned me to him and took my hand. His hold was firm, yet gentle, especially when he lifted my hand to place it over his heart. I felt it beating steadily and it was reassuring.

"He must have said something about the three of us claiming you," Rhys added.

I nodded, remembering the crude words.

"Tell us," he prompted. I glanced over my shoulder at Cross and Simon and saw that Ian was with them as well, although he stood back about twenty paces beside his horse.

"That Simon would share me with both of you as part of the arrangement. Payment."

"Do you believe anything that bloody fool said?"

I shook my head vehemently. "No!" I cried, worried they'd assume the worst of my imaginings. "I discounted him right away, but he grabbed me, said that he'd...he'd have me since I fucked three men already."

The men's spines straightened and their fists clenched.

"I fought him and then kneed him...him in the cock. I got away and took the horse to find you. I needed to be with you." I stepped out of his hold and put one hand on Cross' chest, the other on Simon's as I looked directly at Rhys. "I'm right where I want to be, between the three of you."

They each took a step inward, closing the space between us.

"I love the way you bicker and argue with me," I told Rhys. "I also love the way you have such focus and precision when you touch me, as if every move you make is deliberate and you know just how to bring me pleasure."

I turned to Cross and looked into his green eyes. "I love the way you make me smile, the way you poke fun at my city ways." The corner of his mouth turned up. I felt Rhys' hand on my arm, stroking it, as if he couldn't keep his hands off. "I also like the way you claim me with such inventiveness, eager to show me new ways to...to fuck."

I turned one more time to face Simon as I felt not only Rhys touching me, but now Cross as well. "I can't stay away from you...from any of you. Simon." I met the warrior's gaze. "There's this...bond that I feel with you, as if I can't get enough, as if I take you inside of me, not just your cock, but *you*. Is it that way for you?" I asked, a tinge of doubt in my voice. Thunder rumbled in the distance.

"Ach, lass, ye are mine."

"You are mine," Rhys added.

"You are mine," Cross agreed.

"I don't want just one of you. Combined, all of you are what I want and need." I looked at each of them in turn. While they were big and brawny and brave, they were also flesh and blood with feelings and their own hurts. While they protected and sheltered me, it was my job to be there for them, in any and every way the needed. "I want to be with you, all of you."

The men's hands stilled as Simon tilted my chin up with his finger. "Do ye ken what that means?"

It meant that I would take all three of them at the same time and one of them would fill my bottom. I clenched there at the thought, but they'd been preparing me for this, not only by stretching me to accept a cock, but to accustom me to the incredible feelings that could be found with something there, whether it be fingers, a plug or even a cock. They'd played with me so that I would *want* it, to need to feel that good.

"It means I belong to all of you. Not one at a time, but all of you at the *same* time, for that's how it is, in here." I placed a hand over my heart.

17

$\mathcal{S}$IMON

Two hours later we were home with Olivia settled in the bath, steam rising up from the water that didna hide her body from our gaze. This wouldna be a simple fuck up against the wall, this would be a claiming and it needed to be done right. That began with getting our woman clean and comforted after her ordeal first. My cock wanted to rush, but it wasna the time to do so.

She rode with Rhys, sitting on his lap as we rode back to the ranch. While I didna wish to take my hands from her, I knew that my need for her was too great to hold her so close. I was afraid I might hurt her in my intensity. Just the feel of her soft skin, the smell of her would be too much.

Ian had led the new horse—thankfully we hadna shod the horse's back feet yet—back to the ranch ahead of us to let everyone know Olivia had been found. He would also lead a group that would track Peters and take care of the bloody bastard once the storm blew past. I had a good idea what they'd do with the man and would make sure no one would see him again. While I wished to be the one to finish him off, it was my job—*our* job—to take care of our wife before anything else. Besides, if word of Peters' demise got back to Olivia, I didna want her to have the weight of her men committing murder upon her dainty shoulders. Nothing would come between us now. Nothing.

"You have nightmares," she stated baldly, skimming her hand over the surface of the water, her beautiful pale eyes on mine.

Rhys, who was selecting a plug from the shelf, turned.

Cross paused in unbuttoning his shirt.

Keeping my past a secret wasna easy, as Olivia was verra receptive, and also the first lass with whom I shared a bed. I could hide it while I slept alone, but not when I held her all night in my arms. I must have had a nightmare and nae remembered.

"Aye."

"You all seem to be haunted by events in the past," she added. Thunder rumbled in the distance while the rain continued.

"I grew up in an English orphanage," Rhys confirmed, his mouth a grim line. "Life was...bloody horrible. Then, in the army, we saw terrible things."

"I grew up with a father who liked to use his fists," Cross shared. "Then there was the war. I fought for the North." His mouth formed a grim line.

Olivia watched closely as the men—my true brothers—bared their souls. If Olivia wanted us to claim her, then we needed to give her everything, to share our darkest of secrets. It was time.

I picked up the washcloth from the floor and dipped it in the water. "I was responsible for a girl, for protecting her, but I failed. She and her family were murdered by our commanding officer."

Sadness filled her eyes, so I shifted my gaze to the soap, which I picked up. "Alea?"

I lifted my head in surprise, but I shoulda known she'd seen one of my nightmares. "Aye, lass."

"Did you love her?" Olivia whispered, worry etching her face.

"Nay." Shaking my head, I told her, "She was too young to even consider, but she was my charge and I let her down."

"You weren't even on duty then," Rhys added. "It wasn't your fault. It was Evers. You can't let it haunt you this way."

"I canna control my dreams," I replied, knowing they came to me unbidden as I slept.

"I'll be there to help," Olivia offered.

I ran the washcloth over her shoulder at her tender words. "Aye, lass, ye are there to help, but ye canna share my bed every night. Ye have two other husbands to tend."

"Now I know though, and we can share the burden, the pain, together," she added. "And, I will—from now on—be quite easy to keep safe."

She grinned impishly, for I knew her words were in jest, for it seemed danger followed her everywhere.

"Verra well, I'd like that," I replied. Perhaps her knowing my past could help heal it. If not, I could pull her close and hold on. "Ye, lass, have some worries as well."

"We must know all your secrets, love, to make you happy," Rhys added, holding one of the plugs he made in his hand. Olivia's eyes dropped to it and she frowned, but I took her chin and turned her to look at me. Rhys would play with her arse soon enough.

"I worry you will leave me," she admitted.

I couldna felt more surprised. "Leave ye? Impossible."

"Who's left you to make you feel this way?" Cross asked. His shirt was now off and Olivia's gaze raked over his exposed body.

"My parents died. While it wasn't their fault and I was fairly young, and I felt abandoned." She took a deep breath, which made her breasts rise above the water line. Her nipples were plump and full and I was verra eager to taste them. "Uncle Allen, though, he has his own family. Now that he's shared his secret, he doesn't need me. I don't have a home anymore."

I stood and took Olivia's hand, helping her up and out of the tub. With a bath sheet in hand, Cross came over and began to dry her. "Your home is here at Bridgewater, with us. Your uncle didn't abandon you; he kept a home with you until you had another. We'll go see him in the next few days."

Her eyes were half lidded as Cross stroked the bath sheet over her body. "How...I mean, I thought it wasn't safe with Mr. Peters."

"I dinna ken how he found ye here, but dinna worry, the other men will find him. He willna be a problem for ye any longer."

She looked at me in surprise, but remained silent, for she knew she lived now with a group of warriors.

"Enough about Peters. It's time to make you ours," Rhys said with finality. It seemed he was as eager as I to talk nae more about the arsehole Peters.

RHYS

We saw the horse from a distance, the prairie so vast and treeless. Even with the roiling clouds and wind, it was like a beacon on the horizon. Thankfully, the storm hadn't delivered any rain, otherwise we never would have been able to see her. I didn't want to think about what could have happened to her if the storm was more severe. When I saw she was whole and uninjured, I was able to catch my breath. And it was only when we had her in the bath and I was readying another one of my handcrafted plugs that I relaxed entirely. Tonight, we would claim her together and there would be no doubt, nothing between us.

We'd worked her arse to accept the smallest plug, then two larger ones and she should be prepared for our cocks, but I wanted to make sure she was not fearful of it, for we only wanted to give her pleasure. That was why I selected more of a play plug than one that was for training her arse.

"Grab hold of the side of the tub, love," I told her once she was dry. Her hair was up on top of her head, secured by pins, but the long tresses would come free soon enough. She did as bid, and then looked over her creamy shoulder at us.

I groaned at the sight of her; the long line of her back, her breasts that swayed beneath her, her lush hips and perfect arse— an arse that would soon belong to us. For now, we would make her come from being played with there, so she would know how incredible it would be once a cock was buried deep inside her.

I held up the plug I'd prepared. It was slickly coated with ointment, a very narrow tip that widened into a small ball shape, then narrowed, then widened into a slightly larger ball shape, then narrowed, then again in the same way two more times so that there were four humps that would stretch her arse wider and wider going in, and when she came as I pulled it out.

Cross and Simon moved to stand on either side of her and began running their hands over her, each cupping a breast, tweaking or pulling on its nipple, kissing her shoulder, running a hand down her back. They lavished her with attention as I nudged her legs further apart so that her pussy was on perfect display. I stroked over her soft petals, opening them so I could dip a finger into her to test her readiness. There was no need, for she was glistening with her arousal and my digit came out slickly coated. Placing that hand on a soft globe of her arse, I spread her open so her rosebud was exposed. So perfect and soon, she'd have a cock there.

I handed Cross the plug so I had my hands free to pick up the jar of ointment. After dipping my fingers in, I began coating her opening with it, making her nice and slick on the outside, then beginning to push a finger in, spreading it within as well. Again and again I did this, collecting more ointment and working it into her until she was slippery inside and out. She gasped as my finger breached her, but quickly started to shift her hips back, pushing me further within. Once she started to fuck my finger, I took the plug back from Cross.

I placed the narrow tip of the plug to her opening and began to push it within, turning it back and forth as I did so. Slowly, her body accepted the plug, stretching around the first rounded shape, then pulling it in as it tapered down. I assessed Olivia's body, her breathing, the way she gripped the tub, the sheen of sweat on her skin. Simon looked at me and nodded, then turned his head back to whisper in her ear. It was too quiet to hear, but she moaned and clenched down on the plug in response to his words.

I continued to push the plug forward, stretching her wider with the next rounded section until she opened even further and then tightened around it when it narrowed again. I did that two more times until the plug was all the way in, perhaps four inches long. While it had a wide flange for me to hold and to ensure it would not go in any further, I would not leave this one within. It was a different kind of training plug. This one would teach her the feelings associated with arse play and fucking and would most definitely make her come.

"Such a good girl, taking that plug," Cross crooned. "When Rhys pulls it out, you're going to come so hard."

Olivia was so responsive and with three men tending to her, she would be well satisfied within a minute. With that goal in mind, I dipped my fingers back into her pussy and found her dripping wet. "She loves it," I told the others, and Olivia shifted her hips, the sway making her pussy and ass moving just right.

"Please," she begged.

I smiled, thrilled that she loved it when her men worked her body.

"Are you ready to come, love?" I finger fucked her, ensuring my thumb rubbed over her clit each time I moved.

"Oh, oh God. I need...I—"

"We know what you need," Cross said and I watched as his fingers rolled her nipple, and then gave it a little tug.

Her breath hissed out, but her pussy clenched down on my fingers so I knew she loved a little bit of pain along with her pleasure.

"I'm going to pull out the plug and you're going to come."

"Rhys, I...it's so big, will it—"

I cut off her question. "You're going to come," I repeated, continuing the movement of my fingers in her pussy.

Tugging on the plug, I watched her arse stretch around the largest of the round sections, then close back up. She tossed her head back, eyes wide and screamed. Her hips thrust up as I pulled on the plug again, this time her body easily opened and closed for the smaller round shape, which I knew rubbed over very sensitive flesh, which prolonged her orgasm.

Cross and Simon played with her breasts as she came, my fingers curling and rubbing over the special spot inside her pussy, tugging once more, the plug pulling out even easier.

"Rhys, I...it's too much, I...oh it's so good," she gasped.

With one last tug, the plug came free and she was still coming. I stepped away from her so she was completely empty, Cross lifting her up and carrying her into his bedroom. When he placed her on the bed she was wilted and still lingering in the glowing after effects of her pleasure. She was so beautiful like this, and it made my cock ache, knowing we could do this to her. It was so powerful to be able to use our dominance for good.

My balls were tight against my body and they ached with need. As I watched her with one leg bent so her pussy was on display, I stripped, as did the others. I moved to lay down on the bed as Simon lifted her up and easily placed her so she straddled me with her knees on either side of my hips. She placed her small hands on my chest for balance and I felt her arousal coating my lower belly. My cock slid up the seam of her arse.

"Lift up, love, I've got to get inside you."

Coming up off my legs, she hovered over my cock, aiming now straight for her slippery pussy. Putting my hands on her hips, I guided her back down and moved her until I nudged at her opening. It was so hot and wet I knew once I released her, she'd sink right down onto me. Lifting her head, she met my gaze and held it, tilted up her chin as she shifted her hips as if to shake my hands off. Gladly, I let go and she seated herself. Her eyes flared as I stretched her and filled her. My belly tensed and I hissed out a breath as her inner walls squeezed me, so hot and perfect. When she sat perfectly upon my lap, she held still and whispered a simple, "Oh."

I grinned wickedly, recognizing that this was the perfect connection, but I couldn't remain still, so I thrust my hips up, nudging her womb. "Crammed full, love." A shy smile formed on her lips. "Come here." I crooked a finger and she lowered herself down so I could kiss her, cupping the back of her head.

Once she was in position, Cross and Simon moved, Cross behind her—he'd be the one to claim her virgin arse—and Simon off to her side so she could suck his cock. I let go of my hold and she lifted her head so her pale eyes were close to mine.

"Look," I turned my head slightly to see Simon's cock just by her shoulder. "Simon needs you."

She licked her lips and turned toward him, her tongue flicking out to lick over the head, cleaning it of the weeping clear fluid.

"Good girl, lass, open wide to take me. I canna wait to feel your mouth around me, have your moans vibrate on my cock. I'm going to come right down your throat."

"She just got wetter," I commented, sliding in just a little bit deeper and I thought my eyes would roll back in my head. "Cross, get in that virgin arse of hers and join us. I don't know how long I'll be able to hold out."

18

Olivia

Rhys' thick cock was deep in my pussy and Simon's stretched my mouth wide. I wanted to please them, all of them, and yet they were the ones giving pleasure to me. Rhys knew how to work his cock to make me come and yet he held back as I gladly sucked on Simon, trying to work him and pull his seed from him and swallow it down. I wanted him to be so lost in the pleasure I wrung from his body that he forgot all of his worries. When his fingers tangled in my hair and tugged at the strands, elation coursed through me.

"I'm all slick, love, and should slide right into this delectable ass of yours," Cross murmured, his hand on my hip, his cock pressing against my back entrance. While he stretched me wider than any of Rhys' plugs, he slipped past the fighting ring of muscle easily enough. "Jesus, she's so tight."

I *was* so tight, so full, feeling both Cross' and Rhys' cocks

136

within me was unlike anything I'd ever felt before. Rhys held still as Cross started to pull back then forge ahead a little at a time, and I couldn't help but groan. The sheer bliss of his cock rubbing over the same places as that ridged plug had me ready to come. It was a different feel, an amazing feel and I wanted it so badly. I was close, so very close, but I needed Rhys to move as well.

"Whatever you did, Cross, do it again. She loved it and she took my cock in even deeper. Holy hell, look how full ye are, lass." From his position on his knees, Simon could no doubt see how I was well filled with cock.

I felt Cross press his hips against my bottom.

I was full, so incredibly full. I couldn't be in any more full.

"We're going to move, love," Rhys said as Cross pulled almost all the way out. "You can come. Again and again. Just feel."

I cried out when Cross thrust back in and Rhys pulled back, then alternated back and forth, fucking me in alternating thrusts. I was officially, completely and totally theirs. There was nothing between us, no one to separate us. We were joined and I was the link that connected us all. Mr. Peters nor my uncle nor anyone else could separate us. There was nothing I could do but feel, just as Rhys had said, and I became lost in my men, lost completely. My skin tingled, my body hot, sweat dripped down my brow, my pussy and bottom clenching tightly on the cocks that filled me. One last shift and I went over the cliff, pushed by three strong men into a never-ending abyss of pleasure. My inner walls rippled around Rhys' cock and I clenched hard on Cross with every thrust and it continued my pleasure. I couldn't cry out, as my mouth was full of Simon's large cock. I reveled in it, got lost in it and I knew I had nothing to fear, for my men were there to catch me. They would always be there, always filling me up.

Simon's fingers tightened against my scalp and I knew he was close to coming. I flicked my tongue up and down the bulging vein on the underside, then along the sensitive ridge at the flared head. "Aye, ye are a bonny lass," he growled as his hips bucked forward and I felt his hot seed against my tongue, salty and tasting solely of Simon. Pulse after pulse it filled my mouth and I swallowed to take it all. His fingers loosened on my hair and he slowly pulled from my mouth as he pushed out a pent-up breath.

With my mouth empty, I was able to turn my head and glance back at Cross, then down at Rhys. My pleasure had my eyes blurry, my muscles relaxed. Both men, however, looked tense and driven, as if their pleasure was close at hand and they were using my tight holes to come. I was more than fine with that, for I'd used all three of their cocks for my own. And I wasn't through. As they continued to pummel me, for their pace and intensity had risen, my pleasure, which hadn't fully ebbed, built back to life, like an ember and a strong gust of wind. I was once again on fire, but this time, I could tell them about how I felt.

"It's...oh, it's so much. I'm so full I'm going to...I'm going to come again!"

I tipped right over the edge and arched my back, my muscles tightening as my cry got caught in my throat.

Rhys thrust one last time and grunted, and I felt as his seed filled me. Cross was quick to follow with a shout, both cocks buried deep within. I couldn't do anything but slump down onto Rhys' solid chest and I could feel the frantic beat of his heart.

Cross slowly pulled from me, then Rhys directly after, and I felt both men's seed dripping from me. I was sore, but I knew I was well fucked. I was lucky in that I had not one man, not two, but three who wanted me, needed me, and truly possessed me.

Thunder rumbled, coming closer, the rain still pounding the roof. In my passionate haze, I hadn't heard any of it. Nothing existed outside of these three men's arms.

"I love seeing your pussy like this," Cross said, his finger gently stroking over my tender, swollen flesh.

"We filled you up, love," Rhys said, his hand stroking over my hair.

"We made a babe, lass, there's nae question if it was just now, or one of the many times we fucked ye this week. I canna wait to see you swell with our child, to see the dark haired wee lassie at yer breast."

The idea of making a baby with them warmed me to my soul. Had they filled me with enough seed to make a baby? The vehemence of Simon's words had me believing him.

"What did your uncle call it when you knew you met the right person?"

"Lightning," I mumbled.

Rhys rolled me onto my back so I had three men looming over me, their gazes raking over my body. I could only imagine how slaked and well used I looked and I didn't mind at all.

Rhys' dark eyes held mine as a bright streak of it slashed across the sky, followed a few seconds later with a clap of thunder. "Lightning," he repeated.

I grinned, for he was right. It was as if it was all meant to be.

"Nay, just lightning. Love, too," Simon said, his dark, intense eyes roving over my body then meeting mine. "It's love."

Cross agreed. "Lightning and love."

They were correct. It was lightning and love.

WANT MORE?

––––––

Read an excerpt from Their Treasured Bride, book 4 in the Bridgewater Ménage Series!

––––––

EXCERPT - THEIR TREASURED BRIDE

REBECCA

The journey had been long. If I were to pen a letter to a dear relative, it is what I would write. One never complained or shared discomfort, especially when the missive would not arrive for months. Based on the disaster and ensuring delay, a letter would have arrived in the Montana Territory faster than I. Ever since Chicago, I had ridden alone, no chaperone. It would have been best if I had one, but there was no one I knew who wished to venture into the wilds and unsettled land of the Indians. I didn't wish to venture there either, but the choice was not mine to make. And so I rode up on a borrowed horse to not be greeted by my husband, but a ranch hand. He'd directed me to the largest of houses dotted across the almost treeless landscape.

This time, when I slowed my horse, I was greeted not by one man, but many. I had no idea which belonged to me or—more accurately—which one to whom *I* belonged. Several had dark hair, some had fair, another had the coloring of ginger, yet all were large, well-muscled and decidedly handsome. These were not the usual men who moved within my father's circles in the London elite. They were direct in their gazes, powerful in their stances and looked as if they *lived* life instead of watching it from the outer fringes. These men got their hands dirty instead of paying someone to do it for them. This made them formidable and quite daunting, as I had not been taught how to handle such dominance. One of these men was my husband? My gaze shifted from one to the next, but no one stepped forward as if expecting me. Perhaps I had travelled faster than a letter after all.

One man descended the steps from the porch and approached. "Good afternoon."

"Good afternoon," I replied with a slight nod of my head.

Four women, with curious yet engaging smiles, joined the men on the porch.

"Welcome to Bridgewater. I'm Kane," the man said.

I nodded once again and clenched the reins in a tight grip, hopefully my only outward sign of nervousness. *This* was the moment, the moment I'd been anticipating for three months, and I was terribly nervous. I couldn't be shipped back to England, for I was legally bound to one of the men in this group. Surely, he wouldn't reject me and send me home in disgrace? Could he? I was to live here, in a land so foreign from my own, and in this moment, I couldn't decide which fate was worse.

"Mr. Kane, I am Rebecca Montgomery. I am here to meet Mr. McPherson."

At my pronouncement, two men stepped forward. Both were fair-haired and of similar appearance for it to be obvious they were related, although one was slightly taller, slightly broader, slightly more intimidating and he set my heart aflutter. It could have been because he stared at me in such a way that had me thinking he could see all the way to my soul. While the look was intense, I felt as if his interest was solely on me. If a gun went off, I doubted he would blink.

"Which McPherson are ye seeking, lass?" This was from the shorter of the two men, his voice was deep and clear and amused. His question had me tearing my gaze away from the other.

I swallowed, for it seemed my husband was one of these two.

"Mr. Dashiell McPherson."

"What would ye be wantin' with him?" the brawny one asked. The sound of his thick Scottish brogue had goose flesh rising on my arms and I wasn't even cold.

I looked in his pale eyes, ignoring everyone else, and licked my lips as I tilted my chin up a notch. "He is my husband."

Both men's brows went up at my words, clearly surprised by the statement.

"And how have you become wed?" Mr. Kane asked from my side. He, too, was curious, as were the women who were whispering to each other. Besides a surprised look or two, the men were more reserved in their emotions. Had a woman come claiming to be a bride before?

"It was seen to by my brother, Cecil Montgomery."

"Ah yes, Montgomery. A verra good officer," the shorter Mr. McPherson replied, stepping back. "While ye are quite fetching, I have claimed a wife already." A lovely woman with dark hair came down the steps to join him. Clearly, she was his wife and making that known. He wrapped his arm about her waist and kissed her on the forehead, but he gave me a wink.

"That leaves me, lass." I turned to look at the man who made my heart beat quickly. "I am Dashiell McPherson." While the married McPherson was quite attractive, it was the one before me now who had my breath quickening, my palms sweating beneath my gloves and butterflies taking flight in my belly. His hair was a dark blonde, cut short on the sides and longer on the top where it fell over his forehead. His piercing ice blue eyes held mine, and I felt like a bug pinned to a tray. "Perhaps ye can explain yerself, for I most certainly would have remembered a wedding night with ye."

———

DASH

I hadna expected to become a married man over lunch. This woman was no small slip of a thing. She sat as if she had a fence post for a spine. Her dress a dark green that set off her dark hair, and with her pale skin and lush curves, she was verra fetching. Bah, she was beautiful. It was her eyes though, even beneath the wide brim of her hat, that spoke words she didna. She was afraid, yet the resolute tilt of her chin belied her bravery to ride up and claim a groom. Her accent was of a well-educated, highborn Englishwoman.

At my more crudeness, her only outward reaction was a slight narrowing of her eyes.

"Where is your brother?" We all liked the man well enough to write and invite him to join us here at Bridgewater. He hadna been part of our commanding officer's deceitful and deadly acts, and had been able to return to England and his life without being stripped of rank or of character. We'd hoped he would join us and it appeared he was following through with that very intention, but we didna know he would bring a sister along.

Her chin tipped up even further. "He is dead." Her words were clear and did nae hold a hint of mourning.

Montgomery was dead? She was much younger than her brother, perhaps by fifteen years or more, and hadna been mentioned during our time in Mohamir. She would have been a child then. Perhaps from a second marriage for one of his parents and tucked safely away in the nursery? "Ah lass, ye came all this way on your own?"

The verra idea set my teeth on edge.

"Not the entire journey." She shook her head. "He died in Chicago."

"How?"

"He fell from his horse. It was nothing, at first," she explained. "He laughed it off as he was not one to be injured upon a horse. A day later, he became feverish and unwell. The signs of some internal damage were obvious and he knew of his demise."

She looked down at her gloved hands holding the reins, and then lifted her gaze to mine.

"We were not close, but he felt some protectiveness toward me, for he'd taken me from England with him. Once he knew he was dying, he didn't wish to leave me alone without some kind of security, therefore in the short time he had remaining, he wed me to you. A proxy marriage."

"And you consented?"

"My...my choices were limited," she replied.

Limited, or none at all?

"Did you have a chaperone for the remainder of the journey?"

She looked as if I'd questioned whether the sun set in the west. "Of course, I had a chaperone. Mrs. Tisdale—a woman from Chicago—escorted me the length of the journey until we descended the stage in town. She would have joined me for the final leg to Bridgewater Ranch, but she didn't wish to remain in such a barren environment and was on the stage east at dawn this morning."

Observing the vast expanse of land that was part of Bridgewater as far as the eye could see, the woman's reasoning was valid. It *was* barren. It was one of the reasons the location was chosen by my regimental friends who settled the land originally—

it's remoteness. That was fine for the group of us wishing to remain hidden, but it wasna for everyone. "She was told there would not be another stage for nearly a week and had no intention of missing it."

I could see the woman all but running after the stage to take her away from here. City folk didna last long in the Montana Territory. As for Miss Montgomery—no, it seemed she was Mrs. McPherson now—time would only tell if she'd be able to live in such a foreign land. Her voice had the clipped accent of a well-educated English lady. The way she kept her voice even and almost demure validated that guess. Society life in London was as different to Montana as was chalk and cheese.

"Ye didna wish to return with her?"

She sniffed. "I am not as skittish as Mrs. Tisdale."

Skittish, yes, but also verra brave.

Reaching into the folds of her skirt, she pulled out a folded piece of paper and held it out. "Here."

I stepped closer and took it from her small hand. She was so prim and formal that she carefully kept her fingers from brushing mine even though they were safely covered by kid gloves.

I unfolded the paper and read it. It was indeed a marriage license and it looked official. Folded with it was another, smaller piece of paper.

It was not my intention to die from a fall from a horse! Being in a foreign land and leaving Rebecca alone, I can think of no other way to protect her than by joining her to you. Returning to England is not a consideration, and it is my belief you will treat her well and with honor. While I long to see the vast Montana Territory for which you wrote, it allows me peace in my final moments to know you will protect her with your life. My sister, willful and sheltered, requires a marriage based on

Mohamiran tradition and values found at Bridgewater. I have faith you will see this done.

Your friend,

C. Montgomery

I was married.

When I refolded the letter, I glanced at her. Her expression was controlled and very reserved and *very* English. I'd think she'd be stiff from riding the distance from town. I'd even think her to be wary of so many new faces, but she offered none of her emotions. It was a decidedly British trait, especially of women who were to be an adornment to a spouse and nothing more. If I asked her to her wellbeing, she would, most likely, only provide a passing comment that deflected attention away from her. It was a sign to the type of upbringing she'd had and completely *nae* the kind of woman I would have sought out for a bride.

She would learn that hiding her emotions was nae required, nor wanted. "Unless ye plan to flee now that ye've seen me, let me help ye down."

As she rode sidesaddle, she took my hand long enough to shift her leg over the pommel as I stepped forward and gripped her waist to lower her to her feet. She was lush beneath my hands, her waist narrow by means of a very stiff corset, but I could feel her full hips against my fingers. While she was nay heavy, she wasna a waif either. In fact, she was a perfect handful for a man of my size —and Connor's.

I was verra tall, taller than average, but once standing, she only came up to my chin. She tilted her head back to look up at me over the brim of her hat. I felt her try to step back out of my grasp, but I held her a moment longer than necessary. In that time, I wondered what she'd feel like without the confining stays—if she'd be as wonderfully curvy and lush as I imagined.

Kane led her horse to stand beside the others at one of the hitching rails. We'd come from various parts of the ranch for the noonday meal and would disburse again once we'd eaten.

"There has been a mistake on the paper," I said.

Her eyes widened and she licked her lips. "No, no mistake." Her voice was a little less sure than before.

I held up my hand. "I dinna doubt the validity of this document, nor your brother's intentions behind it in his letter to me. I will honor both. I will honor *you*."

While her shoulders didna droop, I could sense relief in her. Relief nae that we would remain wed, but perhaps more that she was nae being rejected. Thousands of miles was a long way to travel to be spurned.

"The error is that it is solely my name as groom. Connor," I called.

While I kept my eyes on Rebecca, I heard footsteps on the wooden stairs, then across the hard-packed ground. Rebecca's eyes shifted from me to Connor, who now stood beside me.

"May I introduce the former Miss Rebecca Montgomery, our bride?"

"Our...*our*?" She frowned, the first sign of emotion she shared. "I do not understand."

"You are nae just married to me." I tilted my head in Connor's direction. "You are also married to Connor."

Her mouth fell open so I could see a straight line of white teeth as she glanced between the two of us. When Connor nodded his agreement, I saw the color drain from her face and she fainted dead away, right into his arms.

Get Their Treasured Bride now!

GET A FREE BOOK!

http://freeromanceread.com

ABOUT THE AUTHOR

Vanessa Vale is the *USA Today* Bestselling author of over 50 books, sexy romance novels, including her popular Bridgewater historical romance series and hot contemporary romances featuring unapologetic bad boys who don't just fall in love, they fall hard. When she's not writing, Vanessa savors the insanity of raising two boys, is figuring out how many meals she can make with a pressure cooker, and teaches a pretty mean karate class. While she's not as skilled at social media as her kids, she loves to interact with readers.

BookBub

Instagram

www.vanessavaleauthor.com

ALSO BY VANESSA VALE

Grade-A Beefcakes

Sir Loin Of Beef

T-Bone

Tri-Tip

Porterhouse

Skirt Steak

Small Town Romance

Montana Fire

Montana Ice

Montana Heat

Montana Wild

Montana Mine

Steele Ranch

Spurred

Wrangled

Tangled

Hitched

Lassoed

Bridgewater County Series

Ride Me Dirty

Claim Me Hard

Take Me Fast

Daisy

Lily

Montana Men Series

The Lawman

The Cowboy

The Outlaw

Standalone Reads

Twice As Delicious

Western Widows

Sweet Justice

Mine To Take

Relentless

Sleepless Night

Man Candy - A Coloring Book

CPSIA information can be obtained
at www.ICGtesting.com
Printed in the USA
BVHW041641250122
627124BV00016B/1048